Fatal Dec

(The first case from 'The Freeman Files' series)

By

Ted Tayler

Copyright © 2023 by Ted Tayler

All rights reserved. No part of this publication may be reproduced, distributed, or transmitted in any form or by any means, including photocopying, recording, or other electronic or mechanical methods, without the prior written permission of the publisher, except as permitted by U.S. copyright law. For permission requests, contact the author.

This ebook is licensed for your enjoyment only. If you would like to share this book with another person, please buy an additional copy for each recipient. The story, all names, characters, and incidents portrayed in this production are fictitious. No identification with actual persons (living or deceased), places, buildings, and products is intended or should be inferred.

Cover design: - www.thecovercollection.com

A Harmsworth House publication 2023

Books by Ted Tayler

The Phoenix Series
The Olympus Project
Gold, Silver, and Bombs
Nothing Is Ever Forever
In The Lap of The Gods
The Price of Treachery
A New Dawn
Something Wicked Draws Near
Evil Always Finds A Way
Revenge Comes in Many Colours
Three Weeks in September
A Frequent Peal Of Bells
Larcombe Manor

The Freeman Files Series
Fatal Decision
Last Orders
Pressure Point
Deadly Formula
Final Deal
Barking Mad
Creature Discomforts
Silent Terror
Night Train
All Things Bright
Buried Secrets
A Genuine Mistake
Strange Beginnings
Dead Reckoning
A Normal November
Into The Sunlight
Tame The Storm
One True Friend
Whispered Truths
A Morning Murder
Quick To Anger
Red Herring Season
Gathering Clouds
Still Standing

Various titles
Conception- Birth of the Phoenix / A Sting In The Tale

Where to find him
Website & Blog: – http://tedtayler.co.uk
Twitter: – https://twitter.com/ted_tayler
Facebook: - https://www.facebook.com/AuthorTedTayler
Instagram: - https://instagram.com/tedtayler1775
BookBub: - https://www.bookbub.com/authors/ted-tayler

Ted Tayler's Email Sign-up
Want to keep up to date with all the latest news?
Sign up here – http://tedtayler.co.uk

After a brief set of Welcome emails,
a Newsletter will arrive in the 2nd week each month.
I'll only contact you when I have something new to share.
I promise never to share your email address with anyone.

CHAPTER 1

Saturday 28th June 2008

"It's not right, is it?" muttered Daphne Tolliver, "a widespread ground frost last night with the school summer holidays upon us. Global warming, my backside."

Bobby looked up at her from his position on the comfortable couch in their front room.

"Nothing to add, little man?" said Daphne, shaking her head. "Thought not. As long as you get fed and watered, taken out to do your business, you don't give a toss, do you?"

Conversations were limited when you were widowed and spent long periods alone with only a Cocker Spaniel for company.

Daphne Tolliver was sixty-eight years old and widowed a decade earlier. Her late husband, Wally, keeled over in the bar of his favourite haunt, The Ferret in Newton Bridge. It turned out that Cribbage League matches could be as tense as a Champion's League Football Final. Who knew?

Wally's sudden heart attack wasn't fatal, but the induced coma he was treated to on arrival at the Royal United Hospital in Bath only delayed the inevitable. Daphne's younger sister Megan ferried her back and forth to sit by his bedside for five days. Megan never complained, despite the small fortune it cost to park. She knew Daphne would remember to offer to contribute in time. Her sister's head had been all over the place for several weeks. It was difficult enough with time to prepare for a loved one to pass, but Wally's death shocked everyone.

Daphne's parents always showed their daughters the love that went hand-in-hand with being part of a close-knit family. Mum and Dad set the tone while they lived, and the Sumner girls continued the theme throughout their lives.

Both daughters married young. Megan Morris, as she became, raised three children with her husband, Mick. All three were now married, with five grandkids between them. Daphne doted on them, whether children or grandchildren, especially when babes-in-arms.

Daphne and Wally never had children. Not for want of trying. They never bothered to find out whether pure bad luck or a problem with one or the other. Instead, they accepted it as their fa

The couple spent an equal amount of time together and apart, with their various hobbies and interests. Of course, children would have been a bonus, but they had each other, and that was more than many others they could think of who lived around them.

They came from a different generation, her sister Megan often remarked. If couples today had trouble getting pregnant, they called straight round to the fertility clinic chasing an appointment. Always too keen to find someone to blame, Daphne thought. Somehow, she and Wally survived forty years of marriage without extra mouths to feed.

Wally followed his father's trade as a printer. He talked of retiring at sixty-five as his father had done and planned to spend his well-earned leisure days with Daphne. Those days never came. Maybe fewer pints of lager in The Ferret and other pubs might have helped. A Mediterranean diet could have benefited him, too, instead of the traditional English grub that served his ancestors well over the generations.

Days after his sixtieth birthday, he was halfway into his third pint of Stella Artois with the cribbage match evenly poised. He picked up the five cards dealt from the table — the Jack of Spades, the Four of Hearts, the Five of Diamonds. Wally couldn't believe it. He spread the remaining cards in his fingers. It couldn't be, could it? He held the Five of Clubs and the Five of Hearts too. Ever since playing with his friends in this Cribbage League, he'd always struggled to maintain his place on the team. As often as not, he was a reserve and fetched and carried drinks for the warriors at the table.

He had a chance to shine in this vital game within the overall match. He watched the dealer reveal the cut card. Wally's heart leapt as the Five of Spades landed on the table. The highest-scoring hand in this format of the age-old game.

"Come on, Wally," came the cry, "get on with it."

Sadly, Wally's heart didn't carry on leaping. It stopped.

The landlord called Daphne with the dreadful news. She had rung Megan straightaway, and Mick Morris drove them to Bath. They arrived to discover the ambulance still waiting to hand over its patient. The crew inside were working on Wally in the meantime.

Daphne had never accompanied Wally on his nights out with the boys. She preferred to stay at home and watch her choice of TV programme without him grabbing the remote to switch over at a critical moment to check the latest football scores.

As she walked from the living room they had shared for so long to the kitchen, she realised today was another Saturday. When you retire, every day is the same. It's so easy to lose track. When they were first married, Wally played football in the winter and cricket in the summer. Every Saturday, he dashed off with his mates.

Several of those friends were in The Ferret the night he keeled over. He always referred to those occasions as nights with the boys. It was strange to think that each of them had been approaching sixty or a few years older when he died. Yet, because they had known one another for fifty-odd years, they were still boys in their heads. Over the decades, those young sportsmen matured into armchair experts who kept active playing skittles, bowls and cribbage.

Daphne resigned early in the marriage to having three or four evenings every week left to her own devices. Then, of course, there was the cleaning to do, and many a night, she stood as she watched a film while she caught up with their ironing. Megan's little ones enjoyed Auntie Daphne arriving for a spell of babysitting too, so Mick and her sister could have a night out. As a result, filling her evenings had rarely been a problem.

When her niece and nephews grew older, Megan and Daphne travelled into Harrington End for a Quiz Night at the Waggon & Horses or played Bingo in the village hall. A simple life. No dramas. Typical of how country folk muddled through in their quiet corner of the West Country for generations.

Daphne saw clouds gathering as she peered through the glass curtains at the kitchen window on that late June morning. The darker variety that suggested a rain shower might be due. There are no guarantees, except if you decide against a coat or an umbrella. Daphne knew a downpour would start at the furthest point from home on those occasions. Regular as clockwork, just as she and Bobby turned to head home to Braemar Terrace.

The phone in the living room rang. Daphne scuttled back to answer.

"Hello?"

"Only me, Daphne," said Megan, "just checking. Are you still okay for tomorrow?"

"Sunday lunch at the Waggon & Horses?" replied Daphne. "When have you ever known me to resist the chance of enjoying their scrumptious carvery?"

"Righto," said Megan, "we'll pick you up just before twelve. What have you got planned for later today?"

"Keeping an eye on this blessed weather," Daphne told her. "My bet is we'll have a shower this afternoon. I might wait until it's blown over and take Bobby out for a long walk this evening."

"Don't forget to take your umbrella, will you? To be on the safe side," laughed Megan and ended the call.

Daphne didn't admit to her sister that today's extra exercise was the anticipation of another inch on her waistline after tomorrow's Sunday Big-Plate Special. However, it never ceased to amaze her how much food other people piled on their plates. The ones who could least afford to be eating to excess often sneaked back for second helpings.

Daphne was well aware these occasional lunchtime treats were Megan and Mick's way of checking she looked after herself. Not just that she eat a roast dinner on a Sunday, but she wasn't depressed not having Wally around the house. Fat chance of that, Daphne thought.

Phone calls like the one just ended had become the norm following his funeral as Megan suggested new interests in which they both could get involved. Daphne knew Megan meant well. She was just sisterly, but sometimes, Daphne yearned for quiet. That's why Bobby had become so important.

When she and Wally worked, it wasn't sensible to own a dog. It wasn't fair to leave it at home for hours on end if one or both of them dashed out again as soon as they arrived home. So after she retired from her full-time job in the Post Office, Daphne asked Megan to accompany her to the local kennels to pick a puppy.

"I just want a friendly companion," Daphne said, "not one of those ferocious, fighting dogs or one mistreated."

"A rescue dog, you mean?" Megan replied, "I thought you might enjoy that."

"I haven't got the patience," said Daphne. "Something not too big, that's good with children. I couldn't stand the grandkids not visiting because it barked throughout the day, or worse still, nipped at their ankles."

They had spotted Bobby, the Cocker Spaniel, within minutes of their arrival at the kennels in Clatworthy. He gazed at the two humans walking his way and endeared himself to the newcomers. Bobby's amenable and cheerful disposition soon made him a joy in the home. He was never more content than when pleasing Daphne. As the weeks passed, he was as happy to snuggle on the couch with his mistress as he was to race around the garden with Megan's family.

It was only natural Daphne found adjusting to life without Wally difficult. Megan and her family did what they could, and her work colleagues were brilliant in those early months. In a small town Post Office, everyone knew everyone else. So, the posties had a cheery word, and the counter staff did their best to raise Daphne's spirits and involve her in any social evenings they organised. That left other nights and weekends when she might have moped, but Megan usually covered those.

Every Royal Mail branch across the country could have done with more customers in the latter years of the last century, and Daphne's was no exception. The announcement that their branch would close in 2002 accelerated her retirement. That prompted the usual wail of protests from the people most affected. The elderly, the infirm, and those on benefits which could least afford the six-mile bus trip to the next town. They expressed their concerns to the authorities.

Their response was sympathetic, if non-committal. Akin to the now-familiar reaction to sudden death of saying 'sorry for your loss'. After two years with the axe hanging over them, her former colleagues learned they had sold the site. A branch with a much-reduced staff would open in one of the small units in a precinct on the Westbourne Estate.

"Poor devils," Daphne thought when she heard the news, "moving from a popular site on Church Street to a precinct on a run-down council estate.

Daphne wandered from the living room to the kitchen. She had been right; those clouds held rain. It rattled insistently at the windowpanes. She decided to prepare herself a meal and wait for those white, fluffy clouds she saw in the distance to blow across the valley. In an hour, what remained would be a fine drizzle. The sort that hung in the air and got you wetter than a downpour. When she and

Bobby left the house, the showers would be over. Her view of the distant hillside held the prospect of a fine evening.

Wally had always loved this view from the back of the house. He never spent much time at the kitchen sink, where she now stood, but from the upstairs bedroom and garden, the valley stretched before them to the hills separating the town from Shaw Park and Clatworthy.

The couple rented a flat in town for the first two years of their marriage. When they moved to Braemar Terrace in 1960, the two-bedroomed mid-terrace property had been as much as they could afford. They always planned to move to a bigger place. No children meant that a move became a lower and lower priority as time passed. So they stayed put.

Their row of six cottages on the main road out of town had been built just before the outbreak of the First World War. Different neighbours came and went over the years. At the outset, the cottages were occupied by elderly couples in no rush to go anywhere. Their next stop was the churchyard in town or the crematorium four miles away. It was a waiting room. Wally and Daphne used to chuckle over it.

Before they knew it, they became an elderly couple and found the other cottages changed hands more rapidly as younger couples moved in, improved them and turned them over at a profit. Wally didn't see the point of adding refinements to what they had. He was content to keep everything as originally intended. His one concession was to keep it in good decorative order, inside and out.

There were always lots of cars parked outside her front windows these days. Wally cycled to the print works and often when going to his various sporting activities. Wally couldn't see the point in learning to drive. His father never did. He relied on one of his sporting pals to give him a lift when they played out of town. He and Daphne caught the bus if they needed to visit the bigger shops in Bath.

Years had passed since that rural bus service stopped. Daphne couldn't remember when. After it disappeared,

Megan or Mick always helped if she needed to travel further afield.

After she retired in 2002, Daphne realised it wasn't just Wally she missed. She had bought Bobby for the company but felt she ought to do something positive with this spare time. So, she volunteered at one of many charity shops that opened in town. They took in items donated by the public for areas seeking Emergency Disaster Relief.

At first, Daphne worked two hours on a Monday morning. When news broke of a natural disaster on the other side of the world, she joined others pitching in for hours required to cope with the rush. It was heart-warming to see that the British public still dug deep to help those in trouble despite the troubles at home. On Boxing Day 2004, an Indian Ocean tsunami was caused by a massive earthquake. Within hours, killer waves slammed into the coastlines of eleven countries. Despite a lag of up to several hours between the earthquake and the tsunami's impact, it surprised many victims. No tsunami warning systems had been in place. The death toll approached a quarter of a million.

Daphne and the team of volunteers prepared emergency food, water and medicine packs. The donations came from the public and various organisations across the West Country. When the big rush ended, she returned to Braemar Terrace, curled up with Bobby on her lap, and wept.

"I wanted to make a difference, Bobby," she said, "but so many people never lived to receive the help we've sent out there. It was too little, too late. I'll look for something less stressful."

So, she placed an advert in the window of Patel's newsagents, offering a cleaning service. Soon, two other part-time employment opportunities presented themselves.

Despite the massive influx of immigrant labour in the UK's big cities and agricultural heartlands, they ignored this corner of the West Country. There wasn't much call for

Lithuanian car-wash staff in Harrington End. Husbands still washed the car themselves at the weekend or left them dirty.

Daphne noticed the occasional Polish barmaid in the Waggon & Horses, and a girl from the Balkans often begged on the High Street with her three kids in tow. That was the sum of it. It just went to show. The grass wasn't always greener on the other side.

Her advert's first response came from the local primary school caretaker. They wanted someone for an hour every weekday in term time. That little job kept her busy from three to four in the afternoon. Then, one evening, she received a phone call from a lady with a very posh voice.

"Mrs Tolliver, I presume?"

Daphne stood. She wasn't sure why, but lounging in the armchair didn't seem right. The woman sounded positively regal.

"Yes, that's me," replied Daphne, shunning the urge to curtsey.

"Joyce Pemberton-Smythe speaking,"

Joyce was the local MP's wife. Leonard Pemberton-Smythe currently owned the large Manor House that stood a mile out of town on Lowden Hill, a local beauty spot. Her husband benefited from the presumed cessation of gang warfare after multiple deaths in the town in 2001. The murder of Councillor James Crook also helped his cause. But, despite Labour governing the country, pockets of the West Country remained staunchly Conservative. The other parties edged closer to him in that 2001 election, but Pemberton-Smythe survived by the skin of his teeth.

As campaigning for the 2005 General Election began, his much-trumpeted hard-line approach found ready support in the constituency. He promised to take up the cudgels James Crook had relinquished. His constituents confirmed the tide was turning against Labour, and Leonard won with an increased majority.

Like most politicians, he couldn't stop himself from getting his name and face in the media. As someone hot on crime and big on family values, Leonard was invited onto every relevant TV programme plus irrelevant ones.

His wife Joyce explained Daphne's duties, subject to acceptable references. She added that Leonard owned a flat in London where he stayed while the House was sitting. He only returned to the bosom of his family at the weekend. When not required at Westminster in the summer recess, they collected their two sons from boarding school and spent the holidays at their French home.

Alright, for some, Daphne thought when she spotted an article in a weekend supplement two weeks later. The 'little place' in France Joyce referred to turned out to be an eight-bedroomed chateau in fourteen acres of rolling countryside.

Daphne arranged to visit the Manor for an audience with the lady of the house the morning following that first phone call. She wore her best dress and cleaned her shoes. Daphne presumed the elderly gentleman who answered the front door was the butler. For one moment, Daphne thought he was about to send her to the back of the house, to the servant's quarters. But, as she learned later, Crompton was more of a jack-of-all-trades to the Pemberton-Smythes. He allowed himself a brief smile and ushered her into the spacious hallway.

"Welcome, Mrs Tolliver. Your prospective employer is in the conservatory waiting to serve you coffee. It's the last door on the right along the corridor. Good luck."

Daphne thanked him, trotted down the corridor and tapped on the glazed panel of the door. She could see Joyce Pemberton-Smythe sprawled across a rattan chair, reading a copy of Cosmopolitan. When she heard Daphne's tentative taps, Joyce looked over her half-moon glasses and invited her in with a desultory hand wave.

When she left thirty minutes later, Daphne had another cleaning job to fill her dwindling spare time and learned more about the occupants of the Manor House. Crompton, who didn't appear to have a first name, organised visits from gardeners, window cleaners and tree surgeons. He was an excellent chef but had decided that his eyesight wasn't enough to cope with the cleaning any longer.

"We lost a Sevres porcelain vase," wailed Mrs Pemberton-Smythe, "late eighteenth century. It stood on the mantlepiece in the main hall for decades. Clumsy Crompton flicked his duster a trifle too energetically...."

"Oh, dear," Daphne sympathised.

"Smithereens, darling. Utterly kaput."

Daphne promised to take great care of their ornaments. Joyce gave her a look that suggested they were objets d'art, not mere ornaments. Despite that minor hiccup, their conversation flourished. Daphne soon realised the coffee was more for her host's benefit than a means to put her at her ease. She was sure Joyce suffered from a right royal hangover. As for those references? Joyce couldn't wait to agree on terms and ring for Crompton to give her new cleaner a quick tour of the building and return her to the front door.

"We'll see you next Monday then, Mrs Tolliver," said Crompton as they emerged into the sunlight. He walked with her across the patio to the top of the steps to ground level.

"Call me Daphne," she replied.

"Of course," he said. Unfortunately, Daphne received no offer of a reciprocal change of name for himself.

Megan was ecstatic when she learned of Daphne's new appointment.

"Look at you," she chirped, "working at the big house for the toffs."

"It's too big for them," Daphne replied, thinking over what she'd seen on her tour with Crompton. "She's there on her own during the week. He pops in when he feels like it. The boys are away at school during term time. It's not a real home. They've got lots of nice things, but you wouldn't swap what you and Mick have for that place."

"Their money wouldn't go amiss, though," laughed Megan.

Little more remained to be said. Daphne continued to work at the primary school. She moved on from Emergency Disaster Relief to a local cancer charity housed in the Old Police Station. It wasn't as stressful. She volunteered several hours a week sorting through donations of quality unwanted goods, pricing them and dressing the window and store displays. She had performed her cleaning duties at the Manor House except for the holiday breaks. Years later, she wondered how she had the nerve to call herself retired.

CHAPTER 2

Bobby barked and interrupted Daphne's reverie.

It was one of her younger neighbours revving his car engine. A throaty little number it was too. Her brother-in-law, Mick, said it was all fur coats and no knickers. Quite how that related to a car's look and its performance, Daphne couldn't fathom.

"This won't do," she said as she busied herself in the kitchen, "we need to be busy."

The sound of cupboard doors opening and a tap running alerted Bobby to mealtime. He padded through to find his food bowl filled with something interesting. As he made short work of its contents, Daphne placed his water bowl beside him.

She watched her faithful companion double-check that both bowls were scrupulously clean. Then he sat and stared at her.

"Waiting for your treat?" she teased and handed him a dental chew.

That would keep him occupied while she prepared her meal. Her thoughts returned to the enormous lunch awaiting her tomorrow. Tonight, she could make do with the last piece of quiche plus a salad and a slice of crusty bread. That was more than enough.

The evening proved better than expected as the dark clouds had disappeared. The sun kept its warmth late into the evening in June. It was ideal walking weather, so Daphne checked herself in the hallway mirror. A light jacket and a scarf were what she needed — no point changing again today. Her grey hair was shorter these days and didn't need much more than a quick brush. She still treated herself to a dab of lipstick each morning; that was her only guilty pleasure these days.

Daphne's pink summer blouse and navy blue slacks had seen excellent service over the years, but nobody took much notice of an elderly lady walking her dog. If anybody got a second look, it was Bobby.

"Bobby?" she called.

Bobby sighed, left his comfy rug, and shuffled from the kitchen to stand beside her, wagging his tail. His mistress hadn't mentioned 'walkies' yet, but surely they should venture out soon?

Daphne fetched Bobby's lead and attached it to his collar. With a final check that her white chiffon scarf was tied neatly and tucked beneath the lapels of her navy blue jacket, she opened the front door and off they went.

As she left Braemar Terrace, she met the teenage son of Mr and Mrs Brightwell, who lived in the end cottage. He was doing wheelies on the pavement. Daphne needed to step into the gateway of his home to avoid getting knocked over.

"Careful," she cried at the youngster. Carl Brightwell peered back over his shoulder from under his sky-blue hoodie.

"Look where you're going, you old bat," he shouted as he bounced off the kerb and sped towards the town centre.

"Charming, Bobby, isn't he?" muttered Daphne. "Still, we won't let him spoil our walk, will we?"

Daphne Tolliver took the footpath across the meadow and climbed the stile that brought her onto Battersby Lane. Bobby struggled with the concept of stiles and merely ducked under the wooden steps and wriggled through. Daphne had to avoid the lead getting tangled. Once completed, they stood on the narrow pavement on the other side.

Daphne faced two options. They could turn right and make their way across the next two fields. She could let Bobby off the lead there to run free if there were no cows in the field. The farmer knew of the footpath, and an electric fence always kept his herd at least ten to fifteen yards away from any walkers. That wouldn't have stopped Bobby from dashing across to the herd for a closer look. On the other side of those fields lay the main road that led back into town. A well-lit, well-maintained pavement brought them back to Braemar Terrace.

Her second option was to continue with her original plan. Walk through the woods and to thread her way back to the main road via the open grassland of the park. Bobby was soon safely re-attached to his lead. The evening remained warm.

Daphne sensed someone's presence in the shadow of the hedge on the other side of the road. They must have crossed the fields opposite and crossed the stile further up the road.

Simon Attrill was a big boy, but his size and mental age hadn't kept pace with one another. That was how Daphne thought of the poor lad. She always chose to think of people in the best light. He was twenty years old, with a mental age that would be permanently stuck at eight. When she started her cleaning job at the primary school, Daphne overheard several small children calling names as they left the playground, running helter-skelter for home. They were nasty to Simon, who was passing by the school gates.

Simon's parents didn't know how vulnerable his name would make him when they had him christened. It was a freak accident on the slide at the park that altered their lives forever. Simon had clambered to the top, and as he waited his turn, he leaned over the side to call out to his best friend as he ran back to the steps for another go. A moment's loss of concentration and Simon fell to the hard grass surface below, landing on his head.

"Simple Simon," the little devils chanted outside the school gates that afternoon. "Simple, Simon."

The sun disappeared behind a light cloud. Simon's face lit up when he spotted Bobby and ran across the road towards them. It was no surprise that he loved dogs. They were never cruel to him. Simon had heard that Daphne had told the headmistress what had happened that day. The teacher admonished the children, and their parents received a letter. The kids were even nastier to him after that. He didn't go into town in the evenings now. Boys like Carl Brightwell did more than call names if they spotted him. They punched and kicked him and stubbed out their cigarettes on the back of his hands.

"Hello, Simon," said Daphne.

"Where are you going?" he asked.

"We're heading for the woods, and then we plan to walk back through the park to join up with the main road. Bobby hasn't been out for a walk today. Too frosty this morning."

Simon didn't hear her. He knelt on the ground with Bobby slobbering over his face.

"Bobby likes me, doesn't he?" he asked.

"He likes everyone who makes a fuss of him," laughed Daphne. "I'd better get moving. Those clouds are building again. I thought we'd seen the last of the rain for today."

"Rain, rain go away," said Simon.

The big lad stood by the stile and watched the pair disappear towards the woods.

Daphne glanced back as they reached the narrow pathway into Lowden Woods.

Simon Attrill hadn't moved.

"Such a shame isn't it, Bobby," she said, "not a bad bone in his body. There's no justice sometimes."

Bobby had forgotten Simon already. He strained at his lead as dozens of unfamiliar and exciting scents reached his hyper-sensitive nose.

The leafy lane burrowed its way through the many acres of well-established oak trees populating the lower reaches of Lowden Hill and weaved through more recently planted beeches and sweet chestnuts. The gathering clouds added to the gloom as Daphne and Bobby walked further from the roadway under the overhead canopy of branches in full leaf.

Daphne wasn't unduly worried. They used this route in the past when time allowed. She had Bobby with her; nobody else was in this part of the woods. But, since they left Battersby Lane, the silence had been deafening.

Another two hundred yards and they would reach the open ground of the municipal park. No doubt there would be others enjoying the summer evening. Even if they, too, were keeping a weather eye on those clouds. No cause for concern.

Bobby stopped dead in his tracks. Was it a strange smell or a noise he didn't recognise? It certainly unsettled him. Daphne also sensed someone ahead. Not in the lane. They were somewhere to her left. Close by but hidden from sight. She was sure it was two people. Those weren't words she could hear. They were more urgent, guttural grunting sounds.

Daphne couldn't resist pushing through the undergrowth, even though she dreaded the sight that might confront her. She dragged a reluctant Bobby, who seemed to understand nothing good lay behind those bushes and brambles.

Meanwhile, Holly Dean was dealing with her little Princess in the park. They had left her parents' home on the Greenwood Estate twenty minutes earlier at seven o'clock. The twenty-year-old shop assistant planned a brisk walk around the park with her Bichon Frise puppy before the rain returned. Her little bundle of mischief had done its business. Holly was dutifully dropping the waste bag into the bin by the side of the path when she thought she heard a scream.

Holly looked around her but couldn't see anyone in trouble nearby. She saw other people in the park, further away, who now looked in her direction. No doubt, they also wondered what they thought they had heard. Holly realised the noise must have come from the woods. She turned towards the tree-lined path and took a few tentative steps, clutching Princess to her chest.

The rain began to fall once more. Holly hesitated. Should she run home now? It might not have been a genuine scream — just teenagers mucking around.

The second agonised scream sent shivers down her spine.

Holly swallowed hard and bravely trotted into the lane. The rain was coming on harder now — an absolute downpour. The canopy of branches stopped Holly from getting drenched, but behind her, she heard the excited shouts of other park visitors as they raced for shelter. At first, she could hear nothing except the storm above.

Then suddenly, there was a noise behind her. Someone dashed a hundred yards away from the bushes and headed for the park. Holly turned and made out a figure wearing a blue anorak with the hood raised. She couldn't tell whether it was male or female, but the speed at which they disappeared convinced her they were young.

"Hey," she wailed, "what's happening?"

The lane was empty once more. Holly risked a glance from where the young person had come. She saw nothing. Branches were rising and falling like the wings of geese in flight as they were buffeted by strengthening winds. The grass squelched under her trainers as she edged among the trees.

Another faint noise reached her ears; it sounded like a dog whimpering.

Holly held Princess tighter as her puppy shivered with fright. Holly knew how she felt.

At the edge of the clearing, beyond two mighty oaks, she spotted a Cocker Spaniel, its lead trailing on the ground behind it.

Back and forth, it scampered, urging Holly forward into the open space beyond. In the park, people who were now sheltered under the trees heard the young girl's screams in the distance, and soon several men started running to her aid.

They found Holly Dean, Princess and Bobby standing at the foot of a giant oak tree.

Daphne Tolliver lay on the soggy grass, her unseeing eyes gazing at the heavens.

Monday, 26th March 2018

Assistant Chief Constable Kenneth Truelove sat in his office at the Wiltshire Police Headquarters in Devizes. He had just read through an updated file on a crime that had remained unsolved for far too long. A germ of an idea formed as he reviewed the case; perhaps it was time for a different approach.

The brutal murder of Daphne Tolliver left a lasting legacy in the quiet West Country town. Almost a decade had passed since the frenzied attack, yet townspeople still avoided the once-popular beauty spot where she died. The locals continued to talk about the motiveless attack on the defenceless pensioner. Daphne had been a widow for ten years and lived a quiet life. She came from a close-knit family and gave as much back to the community as she ever took from it. Why on earth would anyone want to kill her?

The ACC was aware some murders went unsolved, and killers got away. However, in the past decade, new scientific techniques offered a way of tracing those that slipped through the net.

Screams coming from the wood were one of the few clues to one of the most gruesome murders his county had ever seen. Daphne was walking her dog through Lowden Woods when someone battered her around the head with a rock. Despite one of the most extensive investigations in the county's history, they never established a clear motive. Finally, the detective in charge, DI Dominic Culverhouse, admitted to the press it may have been a case of being in the wrong place at the wrong time.

A Miss Holly Dean heard Daphne's screams at around twenty-past seven as she walked her dog in nearby Lowden Park. Miss Dean went to investigate and overheard Mrs Tolliver's distressed dog among the trees. She then discovered the bloodied body, and her panicked cries alerted members of the public.

Emergency services arrived and contained the crime scene as swiftly as possible. But, unfortunately, the weather that evening was dreadful, and there was no doubt vital clues got washed away by heavy rain or trampled underfoot.

A huge murder hunt followed, and officers took hundreds of statements, but nobody ever faced charges for the savage attack. Culverhouse focused on identifying a youth seen running into Lowden Park from the woods seconds before Miss Dean found the body. Did Mrs Tolliver know that person? Was it a teenage male or, indeed, a female? Could a young girl have carried out such a vicious attack, and what could have been her motive? The police were baffled.

A witness from Braemar Terrace, where the victim lived for many years, saw Mrs Tolliver walk past her window with her dog, Bobby, just before seven o'clock. The two were a common sight in the neighbourhood. The young mother recalled this occasion because the lad next door, Carl Brightwell, almost collided with Mrs Tolliver as he left his home on his mountain bike.

"They had words," she reported, "but I couldn't make out what was said because of the new windows we had installed in the Spring."

Even ten years ago, Carl Brightwell had a reputation in town for being a little toe rag. He was fast becoming a person of interest to the police. The witness confirmed Carl wore a sky-blue hoodie when he rode past her window. The lad was in town at the time of the murder. Over a dozen witnesses placed him in McDonald's with his mates. They were annoying the other customers, and at half-past seven, the shift manager Kief Dariwhal lost patience and asked them to leave.

As soon as they stood outside in the pouring rain, Carl and his cronies overturned the outdoor furniture and emptied the industrial-sized wheelie bins. They then started throwing chairs against the windows and found it amusing to smear rotting food on the advertising boards. Customers trapped inside with their young children pestered Mr Dariwhal until he rang the police.

The county's finest were busy responding to the incident in Lowden Woods, and two hours passed before anyone visited the fast-food outlet. The Police had ignored a frantic second request for someone to attend.

Before DI Culverhouse moved to Portishead and the Avon and Somerset force in 2013, he organised a reconstruction of the Tolliver murder. Another potential witness came forward. A man bird-watching high on Lowden Hill had seen someone in Battersby Lane. He was following the flight of a sparrow hawk with his binoculars when it swooped towards the ground. He lost it for a second, and as he searched left and right, he spotted a man and woman in the lane with a dog. They appeared to be chatting amicably. The man was playing with the dog. He had no doubt the couple knew one another. The bird-watcher had switched his attention back to his hunt for the sparrow hawk and didn't see the couple again.

Culverhouse knew the man in Battersby Lane couldn't have been Brightwell. The person in the blue anorak in Lowden Woods had to be the killer. His team spent hundreds of hours looking for the suspect without success. There were no other credible leads after five years. The Detective Inspector had given an interview to the crime reporter from the Wiltshire Times.

"We reckon Daphne's killer was a local lad who knew the area well," he said. "Several clothing items are being re-examined by forensic scientists for evidence that we couldn't test for back in 2008. That might lead to a breakthrough. I would urge any of your readers with information about the murder to come forward. In particular, anyone who may have been confided in by the killer since June 2008."

Dominic Culverhouse moved onwards and upwards within months of that interview. His successors had added nothing significant to the case file since that time. There was a report from a national newspaper in which an investigative reporter suggested Daphne Tolliver could have been a victim of a serial killer. He believed there were similarities to unsolved murders in Devon, Dorset and Hampshire.

Truelove had flicked through that article and decided against casting it aside. Like Culverhouse and his murder squad, he believed these deaths were unconnected to the killing of Mrs Tolliver. Whether they were themselves connected was for officers from other forces to determine. The main similarity was that they were women killed while walking their dogs. Their ages ranged from sixteen to fifty. A knife was involved in those other three cases. One couldn't rule out a serial killer using a different method to dispose of this potential fourth victim, but it didn't feel right.

From the outset, the lack of an apparent motive hampered the detectives. Daphne Tolliver's death wasn't a result of a robbery, and there was no sign of sexual assault. She didn't have an enemy in the world if you believed her family, ex-colleagues from the Post Office, and the primary school where she was a cleaner. Add in the glowing terms used by volunteers at the charity shops and in the letter from the Manor House; then, it was certain the lady was loved and well-respected.

So, why did someone pick up a rock and bash in her brains? It was a mystery to ACC Kenneth Truelove. But he knew just the man to unravel that mystery.

Gus Freeman was sixty-one years old. The retired Detective Inspector lived in Urchfont, a village five miles out of Devizes towards Salisbury, where Freeman had worked for much of his career. The ACC knew his reputation as a thief-taker. An honest-to-goodness copper who was considered these days as 'old school'. It wasn't a compliment since it marked them down as a dinosaur. Many other competent detectives had 'not wanted on the journey' tattooed across the forehead. The results were there in the headlines of every daily newspaper to show the folly of that policy.

ACC Truelove knew the tune for the police service's new anthem, but he sometimes struggled to remember the words. If he played things close to his chest, he hoped to convince his superiors that this idea was a modern initiative with all the diversity and forward-thinking they craved.

Kenneth Truelove reckoned Freeman's dogged determination and a knack for winkling out that valuable nugget of information others missed would work well on such a case. But, first, he had to convince the old bugger it was a proper job, not one created out of pity.

Freeman's wife, Tess, died from a brain aneurysm six months following his retirement. He was still coming to terms with his enforced solitary existence. She hadn't had a day's illness throughout their thirty-five years of marriage. The ACC took a deep breath, picked up the phone and dialled.

After four rings, the answerphone kicked in.

"Patience is necessary. One cannot reap immediately from where one has sown. I'm not here, so leave your number, and I'll decide whether to bother calling back."

Truelove shook his head. He knew Freeman's reputation as an oddball, but he had to give him ten out of ten for originality. Then the beep ended the existentialist philosophising, not-so-warm, welcoming message.

"It's Truelove here," the ACC said, "call me when you've got a minute, Gus. I'm sure you don't need a reminder of the number."

The message was delivered. Now he had to wait. An Assistant Chief Constable's duties didn't allow time to muse over Freeman's call message. He had to create the vision and set the direction and culture for the county force. He was part of the Chief Officer Team, building public and organisational confidence and trust. It was the responsibility of that Team to enable the delivery of an effective policing service.

There was never a dull moment, but it was all bollocks.

Deep down, Truelove knew it, but he wasn't old enough to take his pension. Instead, it was time to do a John Redwood and at least try to remember the tune. There were meetings to attend and visions to be created. Freeman would call back sooner or later. Of that, he was confident.

Gus Freeman sat in the lounge of his retirement home. That was how Tess had termed the two-bedroomed bungalow when they moved here from Downton just over five years ago. They had planned for his police career to end as the dinosaurs were made extinct.

Her pastoral role at the Wiltshire College in Salisbury had been something she enjoyed too much to quit for the foreseeable future. The College was formed in 1992 when a College of Art & Design and a Technology College merged. The Campus lay on Southampton Road. It offered degree courses in association with Bournemouth University and vocational courses for school leavers.

Tess was a Wellbeing Advisor and was required to work a combination of twilight and night shifts on a rolling shift pattern. Tess might work from three to midnight or ten to half-past eight, but that never inconvenienced the couple. Before she took on this role, Tess suffered over two decades of Gus being called away at a moment's notice when another crime occurred on his patch.

Anyway, it was only ever the two of them to consider. Neither wanted children.

What mattered most to both of them in their career was job satisfaction. Gus got his pleasure by solving those crimes and seeing criminals in prison. Tess had taught for many years but gradually felt stifled by constant changes in curriculum and teaching methods. She got more fulfilment from providing a safe and secure environment for her students on Campus.

At Christmas and the end of every school year, when many left altogether, she returned home with a hundred cards from students who came to think of her as a surrogate mother. Someone they confided in when things got on top of them.

Tess took it in her stride. It didn't make her any more maternal. She shrugged when scooping up those cards to be recycled.

"I don't think I could even put a face to most of these names," she would sigh. "I was just doing what the job entailed."

Gus wondered how prepared those kids were for the outside world. He could never recall his teachers providing a safe and secure environment when he attended school. He couldn't imagine sending any of them a card at Christmas either. They may not have remembered his name after he left at sixteen. But he would never forget the names of those who wielded the cane with glee or whacked pupils with a blackboard rubber.

It seemed so long ago now. Gus couldn't wait to leave school. After six months labouring on a building site, he'd started evening classes to help gain the qualifications he needed to join the police at eighteen. His father warned him against it.

"You'll never be off duty, son," he cautioned, "and forget any friendships you've formed. They will never last once you put on that uniform."

Gus wanted to prove his father wrong, but he knew he was right within six months. Then, within a year, the opportunity to change things disappeared when his father died of lung cancer at fifty-three.

He completed his training in August 1975, and his first posting was to Amesbury. Two years later, he moved into the City of Salisbury. It was an excellent time to be a young copper on the beat. There was plenty of variety. He was encouraged to take his sergeant's exams. Despite being reticent about his academic prowess, Gus surprised himself by passing the first time and decided he had just been a late-developer. He wished those cane-happy teachers could see how he turned out.

Gus Freeman minded his own business, taking a leak in the toilet one morning when someone stood next to him. They said a vacancy was about to be advertised in the team of detectives.

"You should apply, young Freeman."

"I'm not on the square," he told them.

"Even better," he was told. "Mark my words, that job has got your name on it. Nobody else need bother to apply."

Gus didn't need to be told twice. He grabbed an application form as soon as the advert appeared on the notice board. Detective Sergeant Gus Freeman began thief-taking in February 1978.

Gus met Tess in The Swan at Stoford that summer. He was enjoying a few drinks with colleagues on a warm July evening. Tess arrived with a group of teachers celebrating the end of the summer term. The new one began no more than six weeks later, yet Tess returned to work wearing an engagement ring.

Tess and Gus saved hard over the next eighteen months. She had been a late arrival, and her parents were already in their late sixties. They had next to nothing put by and were unable to contribute much. It seemed they faced a long engagement. Almost two years after they buried his father, Gus stood by the same graveside and watched his mother's coffin lowered into the ground.

"No big mystery to solve for the cause of death," he said to Tess later as they stood in the bar of The Duck Inn in nearby Laverstock. "She smoked forty a day Capstan Full Strength since she was fourteen, the same as Dad."

The modest home he had grown up in came to him in his mother's will. Gus and Tess set about re-decorating and ridding the place of the effects of decades of nicotine. She continued to live with her parents. Times may have changed, but Tess was adamant.

The couple were married in Salisbury Registry Office on Bourne Hill in 1980. The detective and the teacher then manoeuvred through thirty-five years of marriage, avoiding the icebergs that brought disaster to many others on the same journey.

Tess lost both her parents within the first five years.

"It's the two of us against the world then, Gus," she would say whenever a problem arose.

Then, after forty years of service, Gus had been called into the ACC's office. He asked whether he had considered retirement. He was three weeks into an investigation concerning allegations of sexual assault over several years at a care home. It had been a traumatic experience and promised to get even murkier. In a moment of weakness, Gus hinted that once this case ended, he might be glad of the chance to spend months scrubbing himself until he felt clean again.

CHAPTER 3

Tuesday, 27th March 2018

The message from the ACC came as a surprise. Gus had listened to it when he returned home yesterday evening after a tiring day. It made a pleasant change to hear a human voice behind that nagging red light flashing on his phone display.

Gus had been pestered in the past by so many computer-generated calls. He often let the number of stored messages reach the maximum of thirty before blitzing the lot without even a cursory check. The chances of missing a vital call were miniscule. It was almost sure to be PPI; his computer would crash the next day or another wrong number.

There were excellent reasons there wasn't a cat in hell's chance of the first two applying to him. As for the third option, Gus didn't enjoy conversations with people who thought he was their best friend or loved one.

The last episode lasted seven or eight minutes. Time lost; he'd never get back.

"Hello?" he'd answered brightly. He always tried harder to be jovial on a Sunday evening. It made him feel better about not attending church.

"Hello? Is that Dorothy?"

"No."

"Oh, is she there?"

"No."

"When do you expect her back?"

"I don't."

"Oh, has something happened to her?"

"It's possible. Perhaps you should call Dorothy to check."

Gus ended the call and made it as far as the drinks cabinet before the phone rang again.

"Hello," less upbeat this time. More unimpressed of Urchfont.

"Dorothy?"

"Still not here."

"That is 01380...."

"I know my number, and that's not it. You must have mis-dialled."

"Oh, I'm so sorry. I'm sure I wrote it down correctly."

"Don't worry. I think you may have switched the sixth and seventh numbers. Take care when dialling again."

"Thank you. You must think I'm a silly old fool."

"Not at all. Good evening."

He got further this time. As the single malt had slid from the glass and across his tongue, the phone rang again.

"The sixth and seventh numbers," he answered.

"How did you know what I was going to ask?"

"A lucky guess."

"I don't know you, do I? Your voice sounds familiar."

"It may be because we've spoken several times this evening."

"You've been so helpful. Gosh, look at the time. Dorothy will have gone to bed by now. Would you mind doing me a big favour? Could you tell her I can't make our bridge club this Thursday?"

That might be difficult, Gus thought, but the caller had gone. He had poured himself a generous measure. He felt he deserved it. After five minutes of sitting by the phone, he decided it was safe to sit and enjoy his drink undisturbed. That proved impossible.

He wondered how his phantom caller mastered counting cards to achieve a tricky five no-trumps on a Thursday afternoon. These bridge clubs involving elderly ladies were hotly contested affairs.

When he wasn't analysing that thorny problem, he scribbled the names of any potential Dorothy that had crossed his path on a scrap of paper. Women who lived in villages between Devizes and the parts of Salisbury Plain that were covered by the 01380 STD code.

Once a detective, always a detective. No matter how hard he racked his brains, it remained a concise list.

Gus gave up after his second drink and went to bed, having resolved to buy a phone with a caller display. He never wished to entertain another wrong number while at home. Most numbers got short shrift these days anyway, but if they seemed familiar, then he could at least weigh up the pros and cons of returning their call.

Weeks later, on a breezy Tuesday morning, the sun did its utmost to brighten his mood. He had to admit he was intrigued by last night's message. A call back wouldn't take much out of his morning. He planned to get across to his allotment. He needed to continue the work he'd put in yesterday.

They were on the threshold of Spring and a new gardening season. It didn't always feel it earlier in the month when the UK endured the tail-end of 'The Beast from the East'. It had been freezing, with daytime temperatures never getting above freezing. The strong easterly winds had delivered widespread snow to many parts, and as usual, everything ground to a halt.

Three weeks further on, temperatures were on the increase. The longer days triggered new growth, and the majority would survive as long as Gus offered his early sowings protection. This milder, unsettled spell was forecast to carry through into April.

Gus had applied for an allotment soon after moving into the village. Retirement was bound to deliver spare time. He and Tess could only take so many holidays outside of term time at the college, and visits to National Trust properties at the weekend didn't come cheap. They needed rationing.

Events changed that within six months. Although Gus struggled to motivate himself immediately after Tess's death, gardening was therapeutic. The patch of land's solace became crucial in his grieving process.

Yesterday, he had put the finishing touches to his winter pruning and started his digging. There was always something. He wondered again what Kenneth Truelove might want. Gus didn't want it to stop him from getting in his early potatoes.

There was nothing for it. Gus picked up the phone and dialled.

A bored-sounding woman answered.

"Can I speak to the ACC, please?" asked Gus, "I'm returning his call. Ex-Detective Inspector Freeman."

She asked him to hold, then treated him to a quick burst of 'Wouldn't It Be Nice' by The Beach Boys while he waited. Gus held the phone at arm's length.

"Truelove here. Good morning, Freeman."

"The cuts haven't bitten too deep, I see. You've still got a secretary."

"Vera is a Personal Assistant," replied the ACC, "and several of us share her services."

"Things *have* changed since I left."

"It's clear that you haven't, Freeman. You understood what I meant."

"Might I also suggest a change of background music? Something by The Police would be more appropriate. After all, Brian Wilson allegedly took an incredible variety of drugs in the Sixties. Is that the right message?"

"I'm a busy man, Freeman. I called because I have a matter to discuss with you face-to-face. So how are you fixed tomorrow afternoon? Let's say, two o'clock here at HQ on London Road."

"Two o'clock? Do I need to drive there with the traffic snarl-ups that the road suffers? OK, but I might be late. It depends on how I get on with my Ulster Classics."

That comment puzzled the ACC.

"I'm sure that means something to you, Freeman. Get here as soon as you can. I can hardly discipline you. Look, I have a serious proposal to put to you. So, please try to leave the levity in the countryside when you travel in tomorrow."

"Message received," said Gus.

He ended the call. Surely, his old boss recognised levity as a defence mechanism. Kenneth Truelove had been a proper copper before achieving a high rank. Unlike many parachuted into leading management positions with many letters after their name but nothing between the ears.

Forty years of hard graft in such places as the one he was attending tomorrow had worn him down. Retirement should have been the time to unwind and relax with family and friends.

Circumstances dictated he enjoyed neither. A few fellow gardeners he bumped into at the allotments. The window cleaner. Although eight visits a year of twenty minutes maximum hardly constituted a friendship. Still, the lad was never short of a word.

Gus lingered in the hallway and tried remembering where he'd left his gardening shoes. He had already checked the usual places without luck. There was the danger that this time alone had messed with his head. He refused to consider the 'D' word. He banned it from his vocabulary.

Nevertheless, he opened the fridge door and risked a look. See, nothing to worry over, he chided himself. If only Tess were still here. She used to tell him not to leave them where he dropped them on the porch. Gus kicked them off before walking indoors to avoid leaving dirty marks on the hall carpet. He thought that would help.

He opened the front door. Mystery solved.

Ten minutes later, he opened his garden shed to fetch his tools. The allotments stood on a stretch of land next to the Parish Cemetery. Other allotment holders around him were hard at work on their plots. He acknowledged a wave from Bert Penman, a retired butcher, as he straightened himself slowly from tending to his strawberries. A back-breaking job, clearing off old leaves and cleaning the ground between the plants before applying a top-dressing of general fertiliser. Hard enough for a man Gus's age, but much harder for old Bert. He was eighty-five if he was a day.

Frank North sidled across from next door. A weasel of a man who looked like a gust of wind would blow him over. He was in his early seventies and had worked for nearly every farmer in the district at one time or another before retiring last year.

"I'm lighting a bonfire in half an hour. Would that inconvenience you?"

"That's fine, Frank. Thanks for asking."

"I've seen you sitting here of an evening, reading or contemplating life. Do you ever spot anything untoward on the hillside over yonder?"

Frank knew Gus was a former policeman. He didn't engage in conversation much. Gus got the impression Frank thought he'd still have his nose into everything, and retirement never altered how a copper spent his time. Gus shaded his eyes from the sun and stared at the distant hill.

"What am I looking at, Frank? I can't say anything odd has ever struck me."

"I know the area better than you, I bet," said Frank. He sat on an upturned wooden crate and began rolling a cigarette. Whatever the problem was, it would mean a further delay in the Ulster Classics schedule.

Frank was ready to continue. Although what satisfaction he got from the spindly roll-up he now took a drag from Gus couldn't fathom.

"Can you see the clump of trees on the hill? Just to the right of the church tower ahead of us?"

Gus nodded. Frank coughed for several seconds and then continued.

"Behind those trees is a lane that runs along the backs of the cottages on the hillside."

"I didn't even realise there were any cottages, " Gus said. "They're hidden from view by those trees."

"They built Cambrai Terrace after the Great War," Frank continued, "sixteen cottages owned by the council. They got sold off from 1981 onwards, thanks to Thatcher's government. Those cottages are now privately owned, and because there was no gas that far out of the village, most have oil-fired heating or night-storage radiators. Bloody expensive to run. If you could see the roofs on some of them, they've added solar panels to reduce the costs."

Gus let him carry on. He knew why Frank could supply intimate details of these places. He'd done a spot of breaking and entering in the distant past. Hence the reason for so many changes of employer. Frank wasn't fussy about who he stole from or when and had suffered many short terms of imprisonment when he got caught. Which he always did. He wasn't the brightest spark.

"So, what makes you think there's something untoward happening up there, Frank?" he asked.

Frank held up a hand. Gus needed to wait while he coughed again and rolled a fresh cigarette.

"Follow the line across the hillside from that clump of trees until you reach the willows."

Gus followed the direction Frank pointed.

"Willow trees, are they? Difficult to tell from this distance."

"They're osier willows," explained Frank, "the sort you want if you're weaving things like baskets or hurdles. They grow like buggery. Sixteen feet in a year. They end up half as tall again if you don't harvest them."

"Similar to a leylandii, but useful," suggested Gus.

Frank grinned.

"When you're sitting here of an evening, keep an eye on those willows and tell me what you make of what you see."

With that, he got up, stubbed the second thin cigarette out with a boot heel and returned to his gardening.

Gus didn't know what to make of it. Maybe he would drive up there one day. Frank wasn't going to let him into the secret this afternoon.

True to his word, Frank gathered the old leaves and twigs from trees overhanging his plot, plus the results of pruning his fruit trees. Unfortunately, the bonfire took a while to take hold. The tinder-dry kindling he fetched from inside his shed struggled to overcome the dampness of the vegetation. As a result, there were very few flames but an awful lot of smoke.

Gus decided not to hang around to learn which side won out. Instead, he could return earlier tomorrow morning to give himself half a chance of getting two rows of early potatoes into the ground. Then, provided the meeting with the ACC didn't take too long, he could get back to wrapping straw around his plants to protect them in case of frost.

A forecast was just that. The pretty, young TV weather girl promised one thing, and Mother Nature delivered something else entirely. Bert Penman gave him a piece of advice the first Spring he'd worked here.

"Ignore the calendar. In this country, it's best to prepare for the likelihood of getting all four seasons in one day. That way, you won't go far wrong."

Wednesday, 28th March 2018

Dawn had brought the morning Bert Penman predicted. A ground frost greeted Gus Freeman as he walked through the village to the allotments. An earlier radio bulletin suggested this mild spell would bring changeable conditions to the West.

Gus smiled to himself. Just a few words away from the forecast they had issued last evening, and they covered themselves from any admonishment. It was a wonder more weather forecasters didn't move into politics. They could magic up an excuse for any occasion.

By lunchtime, his chores were complete. The Ulster Classics had been sown and wrapped up warm on the off-chance that there was an early nip in the air in the coming days.

Before driving into town, he had plenty of time to prepare homemade soup from his vegetables. So first, he diced the carrots, parsnip and swede and added the vegetable stock. Then, while the machine clunked and whizzed in the background, he cut a healthy-sized wedge from his loaf of wholemeal bread and dropped it into the toaster as the timer reached three minutes.

Twenty-five minutes from start to finish, he thought as he savoured the nourishing snack. Tess would be proud of me. I'll freeze the rest of that batch later, and the four servings will be ideal for speeding up my lunchtime meals when I'm busier on the allotment next month.

Cooking was a skill he'd developed over the past three years. As a beat copper and as a detective, meals had been basic. At home, they were often interrupted by an urgent call from the station. Out on the job, they ate fast food on the run. Not suitable for digestion or the waistline.

All that stopped when he retired. Tess wanted them both to adopt a healthier diet. The premature deaths of their parents had been due to lifestyle choices. Tess admitted that she smoked the odd cigarette in her teens soon after they started dating but didn't continue because she didn't enjoy the experience. Gus had never touched the stuff. Money was tight enough as a teenager without chucking it away.

The allotment was the first step in the search for The Good Life. They dreamed of growing as many vegetables and soft fruits as possible. Now he was alone. Gus didn't want to change that plan. He owed it to Tess's memory to follow through with what she had started.

Gus checked his watch. Despite his reservations, he should get to this mysterious appointment with Kenneth Truelove on time.

He drove away from the bungalow and turned onto High Street. The high hedges on either side of the narrow road screened the red-brick houses with their thatched roofs from the sparse village traffic. There was a mix of social housing and higher-end detached properties on either side of the local pub on the left-hand side. As he drove past the more affluent end of the village and the gaps between dwellings increased, he admired the mature trees and gardens that graced the roadside. It was a pleasant place to live,

He turned onto the A342 and headed towards Devizes. A gaggle of ladies who lunch shuffled out of the Fox and Hounds on his right. Gus hoped they had a designated driver. The place had an excellent reputation for food, though, so he'd heard. If he found someone to dine with, he might give it a visit.

Gus negotiated the multiple series of roundabouts that town planners thought made traffic flow smoother and made his way up the A361 towards his destination. He passed the Crammer on his right-hand side. The name of the famous pond came from the German word for a tradesman. German merchants visited the town centuries ago and set up their stalls on the small green next to the pond. The Crammer was also the supposed site of the Moonraker legend, in which canny Wiltshire smugglers duped the excisemen by hiding their kegs of brandy in the pond and pretending to be raking for the great, big cheese.

The excisemen knew it was the moon's reflection but didn't check what lay beneath the surface. Those excisemen were responsible for Wiltshire folk's reputation since those times.

That they were strong in the arm and thick in the head.

The Wiltshire Police Headquarters loomed on his left. An imposing structure that was built in the early Sixties which. Gus had visited on several occasions. The visitor's car park was well signposted, and he found several empty spaces. He settled his ten-year-old Ford Focus between a BMW and a

Peugeot. They carried a fifteen and a seventeen plate, respectively, but his trusty four-door saloon didn't look too shabby in comparison.

Gus wasn't a petrol head. He only needed a car to get him from home to the shops and back each week. If he did three thousand miles a year, that was a miracle. He used it for an occasional trip to the allotment if he needed to transport any heavy items. He doubted the Peugeot ever carried twenty-five-kilo bags of compost or a bale of straw.

When he reached Reception, he realised several pairs of eyes were studying him. Should he have changed his clothes? Bugger. He was so used to donning things in which he felt comfortable.

His check shirt, sweater and muddied trousers looked okay on the village allotment, but obviously, they were frowned upon here. He almost kicked off his shoes to avoid dirtying the pristine flooring but wasn't sure whether he had holes in his socks.

The officer on duty stepped forward. Gus waited for him to speak, but the younger man merely raised an eyebrow. Such a tiny change of facial expression, yet it conveyed so much.

Gus imagined it meant; are you sure you should be here, Sir? How may I assist you in reaching your intended destination?

"Ex-Detective Inspector Freeman to see ACC Truelove."

With the silence broken, the officer's face went through various changes. It reminded Gus of the old wrappers from a Fry's Five Boys Chocolate Bar. Not the same emotions gained from the popular confection, but certainly, there was shock, disbelief, alarm and a dawning realisation that an apology was the right thing to offer.

"Of course, Sir. We were expecting you. Could you sign in, please? Here's your Visitor's pass. The ACC's Personal Assistant will come to escort you to his office. Please take a seat."

Gus followed orders. At two minutes to two o'clock, a lady descended the stairs. Vera's appearance was a polar opposite of what Gus imagined belonged to the fed-up voice he heard on the phone. She was in her early fifties. She was tall, slim, and with long black hair that shrouded her face as she carefully made her way to Reception.

Once she had accomplished that on four-inch high heels, she looked towards him. Gus quickly closed his mouth. Her eyes were green and bright. Her black skirt was not short, but it did more than enough to highlight her great legs. His initial thought had been slim, but the crisp, white blouse was tailored and hugged her curves. Vera was a beauty. What a crafty old dog the ACC turned out to be. No wonder several of the top brass had dibs on accessing Vera's shared services.

"If you would follow me, Mr Freeman," she said, showing no signs of noticing Gus had been drooling. Vera waited on the first step for him to join her. They were to walk up together, side by side. Gus cursed under his breath. Of course, she noticed. How long was his chin on the floor, he wondered.

Vera ushered him into the ACC's office. His old boss stood by the window, studying the front car park.

"Tea or coffee, Sir?" she asked.

"Tea for me, Vera," said the ACC, "that okay for you, Freeman?"

"Anything as long as it's hot and strong."

Vera closed the door behind her. Gus noticed the briefest of smiles on her lips. Full lips, not too heavily made-up.

"You've kept the Ford Focus on the road then, Gus? Not swapped it in for a Land Rover yet. I thought that was more your farming community types mode of transport."

"Sorry. No, I'm happy with my little runabout. There's been no reason to swap."

"Nasty business on your old patch, Freeman? I never thought we'd be dealing with nerve agents. Not in sleepy Salisbury."

"A sign of the times, I'm afraid, Sir, but that isn't why you brought me here, I imagine?"

Truelove handed Gus two folders. One thin and one thick.

"Everything you need on salaries, forms to sign, official ID and the like are inside, plus the first thing we want you to investigate."

"You appear to have missed out on one important step, sir," said Freeman. "I have no idea what you expect me to consider in these files."

Gus flicked disinterestedly through the thinner file while the ACC stood and walked back to the window. He carried on with his prepared speech without answering.

"You would be assigned to Superintendent Mercer's team."

"Geoff Mercer? A Superintendent. How on earth did he ever reach such dizzy heights?"

"He's a very competent officer," replied Truelove, "who delivers the twenty-first-century policing that we expect from him."

"Heaven knows why I'm here, then," Freeman snorted. "When are you going to tell me what this is about?"

"What this is about, Sir," his former boss cautioned.

"Sorry, boss. I'm out of the habit. Anyway, I *am* out. I'm retired."

"Look, let's cut to the chase, Gus. You're a natural detective who considers a bucket load of facts and instinctively selects the most important, like a prospector sifting for gold. You understand people, whether they're villains or victims. Eyewitnesses tell you things they didn't realise they knew in an interview. Suspects reveal things they didn't want you to learn that they knew. You can't teach that. It's innate. Either you've got it, or you haven't. You have. I never did. Maybe Mercer never did."

Freeman looked about to say something, but the ACC held up a hand.

"Whether you rate him as a thief-taker or not is irrelevant. He's a senior officer, and you will treat him as such. Is that clear?"

"As clear as mud," Freeman shrugged, "you still haven't told me why I have this."

He waved the thin folder.

"As for what's in this weighty tome on my lap, that's still a mystery."

"We need you, Freeman. I'm setting up a Crime Review Team. Its role is to review cold cases with a fresh set of eyes in tandem with our state-of-the-art digital facilities. Our computer whizz-kids will carry out the number-crunching and in-depth search routines for you. Their role will allow a small investigative team under your guidance to take on specific cases that might profit from more old-school methods."

"Superintendent Mercer is in charge of this proposed set-up, I assume?"

"He's responsible for the investigative team. We have a digital support group that is separate and available to everyone."

Gus Freeman tapped the main folder. Before jumping into it, he wanted a clear picture of what was on offer.

"Let me get this straight. I'd review a set of cases and be free to work them as I saw fit?"

"Exactly. Geoff has overall responsibility, but his existing staff comprises small teams that he expects to function without direct involvement."

"Cushy number," Gus said.

The ACC scoffed.

"Come on, Gus. It's no longer a freewheeling force on a jolly. If it ever was. The government's cutbacks have bitten deep. The budget for this Crime Review Team would be small. Most of the County's resources are committed to getting the immediate crime figures under control. Cold cases rarely get a second chance these days. Backroom staff numbers have been cut just as hard as front-line officers. It was a devil's job to persuade HQ to authorise taking on a young graduate to strengthen the team."

"A graduate?" asked Gus Freeman. "What do I want with a wet-behind-the-ears lad that needs me holding his hand? I would need solid, experienced officers."

"I'd better not see you holding hands with this one, Gus. People would talk. She's twenty-five. Well, you'll find out later."

"Can she make a decent cup of coffee?" asked Gus, with a grin that showed he was only taking the piss.

"Yes, very funny. I don't need to remind you things have changed even more in the past three years since you handed in your warrant card. Watch your step. It would be best if you thanked Geoff Mercer for persuading the top brass to take her on. It's getting harder to get youngsters in through normal channels. This channel has opened, and we might encourage the brighter ones to become community officers. Get them in through the back door."

"I can't argue with the logic behind that," agreed Gus. "They can concentrate on prevention rather than actual policing. While they absorb the time-consuming grunt work, trained officers can tackle more serious issues."

Gus considered the implications of accepting the ACC's proposal for a few minutes. Truelove bided his time and said nothing. There was a tap at the door. Vera returned with two teas in delicate china cups and a plate of bourbon biscuits.

Gus breathed in as she swept past him to return to her desk in the outer office. He couldn't place the fragrance. Tess preferred Chloe. Not that he could remember the last time he bought it for her. A bottle lasted her ages. There was still an unfinished one in the dressing-table drawer.

Gus hadn't thrown any of those personal items out yet. The brush still held precious strands of her greying hair. The necklace he'd given her on her thirtieth birthday. Trinkets that reminded him of the exact minute and place he bought them.

Her wardrobe stood empty now, but he'd held back a scarf she loved. Its role now was to cover those personal items in the dressing-table drawer, and in return, he hoped it would preserve the scent of her they contained.

Her clothes had been hard enough to throw out. A lot of them she hardly wore and would have been prime candidates for the charity shops. How was he to know what was saleable and what he should dump? He decided, in the end, to throw everything into the recycling.

That way, there was less chance he'd have seen Frank North's missus strolling through Urchfont village wearing Tess's winter coat.

"I'm not sure I even want to come back to work," Gus admitted. "I take it from the paperwork I'd be working in a consultancy role. I wouldn't hold an official rank. I made it to a full Detective Inspector before I retired. Will this Crime Review Team be my thing? How can I be sure this isn't a pity party? Poor old Gus Freeman. Sat alone with only an allotment to look after."

"It was never like that, Gus. I promise you. We don't get many murders in this county. Despite that, it's raised several questions. Why is the clear-up rate so low? Your attention to detail and understanding of how people tick at every level of society will close several cases after too long. What do you say?"

"There's nothing here to say where we'll work. If I read the brief correctly, I'd have two Detective Sergeants and this girl. Will we have a window out onto London Road too, sir?"

"You must understand, Gus. A new low-priority department has to be thankful for what they can get. Did you ever visit the station where Dominic Culverhouse was based? Or Phil Hounsell before him?"

"I can't say I ever had the pleasure," replied Freeman, "but if I remember right, it was a Victorian building typical of hundreds around the country. They stood on the corner of High Street and Church Street. Right in the middle of everything. Very useful on a Saturday night when the pubs shut and fights broke out. In the Seventies, it would have closed overnight. By the turn of the century, it closed. Replaced by a big, shiny open-plan glass and metal monstrosity as remote from the public as possible."

"There *is* a new building on the town outskirts," said the ACC, "but Mercer has secured you a unit on the first floor of the Old Police Station, as it's now called. There's a Food Bank and a charity shop on the ground floor. As you can tell, there have been a few changes since Culverhouse left."

"Is there anyone else upstairs? How can we keep things secure?"

"The other offices are unoccupied. The authority never sold the premises. We lease parts out. A lift was installed at the rear to allow potential firms access to the upper floor. Other than that, the only structural change involved the removal of the old cells. The new building you hinted at has a modern custody suite, as you would expect."

"Hot showers, duvets and wide-screen TV, I presume?"

"Things haven't got that bad yet, despite what newspapers might have the public believe."

Gus eyed a second bourbon. Vera could make a proper cuppa; he gave her that much. It might be an idea to drop in to see the ACC again.

"How long do I have to think this offer over, Sir?"

"Twenty-four hours. Read the weighty tome tonight and return it tomorrow afternoon. Give me your answer then."

"Will Vera be downstairs waiting for me?"

"Sign in, Freeman. Keep your Visitor's pass and make your way up by two o'clock. I'll get Geoff Mercer to join us."

"Not much point interrupting his busy schedule. I might not be keen on the idea. Plus, if he still has a sweet tooth, the bourbons will have gone by the time I get here."

"I'm confident that what's inside that folder will whet your appetite, Freeman. You'll want to nail the bastard responsible as much as I do."

CHAPTER 4

Vera fixed him with those green eyes as soon as he left the ACC's office. He wasn't sure what she saw. A scruffy sixty-one-year-old widower, or supper?

"Enjoy the rest of your day, Mr Freeman," she purred.

Gus felt the heat of her gaze as he made his way to the ground floor. The officer on duty at the Reception desk glanced up when he breathed his massive sigh of relief at not tripping and making a complete arse of himself.

"Please remember to sign out, Sir," the officer called out. Gus walked across to the desk.

"I'll be back tomorrow. Same time. So, I'll hang on to this pass."

"Right you are. Have a nice day."

Gus sat in his car for a few moments before belting up and starting the engine.

Was it a blessing that if he accepted this consultancy role, it meant working in the next town, six miles away? Or a curse because he wouldn't see Vera with her curvy body and long legs every day?

Why was he even thinking of her? Surely, it was too soon to be thinking of moving on? Tess had been his soul mate. The two of them against the world.

If he'd lost Tess twenty years earlier, finding someone to share his life with might have made sense. He was too old now. He had come to terms with his solitary existence. Only a fool would believe they might attract a woman as beautiful as Vera.

The two folders lay on the passenger seat. A problematic evening stretched before him. He shook his head to clear the memory of Vera's green eyes, which seemed to bore into his very soul. He needed his wits about him. Things promised to be challenging enough without the complications she might cause.

Despite the colder-than-forecasted start, the afternoon now felt pleasantly mild. Although he didn't need to work on the allotment, Gus knew the solace it offered could assist his decision.

He dealt with the soup portions and stacked the boxes in the chest freezer on arrival at the bungalow. Detailed and dated, ready to retrieve when required. As he closed the freezer lid, he considered the ramifications of a return to work.

He had spent the past three years tending that allotment. A peculiarly British tradition carried over from WWII, and the 'Dig for Victory' campaign. Yet, there was a resurgence over the last twenty years of growing vegetables and fruits. Younger faces were dotted around, even here in the village. Bert Penman had probably held his plot for fifty years, if not more. Frank may have only tended his since the last time he came out of prison. No shortage of people wanted to grab a plot when it became vacant. He'd been fortunate the waiting list was short. A brutal winter killed off regulars that Bert had been friends with, and Gus only had to wait six weeks before getting his opportunity. It's an ill wind.

The allotment he took over had been worked regularly by someone experienced — a gardener who had done much of the back-breaking work. Gus spent most of his time deciding what he intended to grow and checking with Bert when to sow, tend the plants, and harvest the crop.

The supermarkets cornered the market in controlling the size and shape of carrots and beans. Maybe an allotment holder struggled to match their price, but you couldn't beat the taste of that first crop of new potatoes you grew yourself. Gus kept a bag of petit pois peas in the freezer. Heresy, really, but peas were a bugger to grow. He'd tried the first year, despite others telling him not to bother. Based on Bert's advice, he'd selected the first pod, which looked mature enough to harvest.

Gus had run his nail along the seam, teased the pod open and gazed in wonder at the six green gems inside. He sat outside his shed, savouring each one, remembering his first experience in his grandfather's garden at five years old.

He had wiped a tear from the corner of his eye.

Bert Penman called across to him.

"Told you. Waste of bloody effort. You'll never get enough peas home to make it worth bothering."

The voice of experience. Gus ripped up the pea sticks at the end of the season and never bothered growing them again. He would never forget the taste of a pea straight from the pod as long as he lived. That was enough. He could cook the supermarket variety with battered cod and a few chips. The fresh ones would be a luxury.

Those experiences were priceless in Gus's mind. Was he prepared to lose them to return to work full time until these potential cold cases got resolved? He couldn't decide.

If he could ensure his trips to the allotment were less frequent at tomorrow's meeting and not stopped altogether, he might work around it.

The ACC's offer couldn't have come at a worse time. This year, everything had been delayed because of the dreadful weather, but his second earlies and first main crops of potatoes needed planting in the coming weeks. He had half a dozen varieties of green vegetables, plus his onions and leeks, lined up to join them.

How many hours must he commit to these cold cases in the proposed consultancy role?

Those matters needed a lengthy discussion tomorrow. Even if the digital support facility the ACC took such pride in covered the research work, there would be dozens of witnesses to re-interview. If they were even still alive after all this time, Gus had sneaked a peek at the dates on the oversized folder. This murder occurred ten years ago; the victim was sixty-eight years old. Time marches on.

He decided to stop agonising over the dilemma for an hour. His mind and body needed sustenance. After a hot meal and a glass of wine, he loaded the dishwasher and left it to do its business. He picked up his evening's primary reading material and wandered to the allotment. Frank's bonfire had expired. Bert was probably tucked up in The Lamb, enjoying an early evening pint after his afternoon's labours. A husband and wife on a patch on the far side appeared to be finishing for the day. They were too far away to notice him.

After he'd unlocked the shed and fetched out his chair and a book, he made himself comfortable. Finally, he had the allotments to himself.

In the distance, he could hear the sound of traffic if he tried. Close by, the sound of birdsong from the trees accompanied his musings. The rustle of tiny animals in the undergrowth on the edge of the allotments kept him company as the sun slid from the sky.

The folder remained unopened on the upturned wooden crate by the shed door. Gus turned his attention first to a dog-eared copy of the journals of his favourite philosopher, Soren Kierkegaard. In the dark days after Tess's death, he searched for answers. Neither of them was particularly religious. Tess had shrugged her shoulders and recounted a comment she had overheard from one of her students back in the day: -

"If there was a God, how come the Pet Shop Boys had a number one hit?"

That had been as deep as their conversations went.

Since her death, Gus needed to explain why it happened *when* it did, only months after the final third of their life together began. The Danish philosopher was a mystery to him when he first discovered the copy he now held. It had been cast aside in an old suitcase stored in the loft along with other textbooks and novels Tess had collected over the years.

She never mentioned it, nor could he ever recall her reading it in his presence.

Gus threw the suitcase and the rest of its contents into the boot of the Focus, and it joined a raft of other items disposed of at the recycling site that weekend. Something stopped him from including this book. What had Tess learned from it? Could it provide clues? He had already found the perfect spot to delve into its contents. Where he sat now, alone in the countryside, next to the cemetery and the green shoots of new life in the soil by his feet.

Kierkegaard explored the emotions and feelings of individuals when faced with life choices. His key ideas included the concept of subjective and objective truths and the three stages of life's path. But there was so much more. Gus realised he had just scratched the surface.

Everything in his life up to his retirement had been about uncovering the truth. To find what the people he interacted with knew of a particular series of events. He concentrated his whole life on understanding people and their motivations. Why did they lie, steal or kill? How was what they said relevant to the case he investigated? Nothing else mattered. Did it mean they were guilty, or had they revealed a fact that showed him the path to finding the person who was?

Gus had copied one quote on a scrap of paper that spoke to him and took it home. He placed it on the table next to his favourite chair. It remained there still, tucked under a coaster. It became a constant reference to how his life might benefit from a new beginning.

'One must first learn to know himself before knowing anything else. Not until a man has inwardly understood himself and then sees the course he is to take does his life gain peace and meaning.'

Gus ran his fingers down the spine of the journals. When did he ever analyse his feelings? What sort of man was he? How did others perceive him? In the line of work he had chosen, it was common for a police officer to be mistrusted, disliked or even hated. Was that solely because of the job? For their part, officers didn't give a toss about what other people thought of them. They developed a hard shell and got on with finding the truth. That became their be-all and end-all. Had he been that way to the exclusion of every other emotion?

Tess had been the only woman he loved, the only person whose opinion of him he ever valued. She loved him in return because he was confident, but did she see flaws in his make-up that she overlooked? She'd never offered an opinion, and he'd never asked. Maybe, deep down, he didn't want to know the answer.

A thought struck him as he finally picked up the cold case folder. Old witness statements and freshly unearthed clues would cloud his musings over such existential matters and the meaning of life.

One consolation was that he was good at those things. He would find the truth in these pages, look deeply into the eyes of witnesses and suspects and learn their secrets — the blood pumping in his veins once more. The hunt would be on. He'd missed that buzz.

Not much had changed in the paperwork he found inside. Most of it was familiar to him. When this murder first hit the headlines, he'd been wasting time with a dispute between neighbours over a boundary fence that escalated to a fight. Not just the husbands but the wives joined in too.

It was clear from the contents of the folder that Culverhouse suffered like so many before him. He couldn't let the case go and probably kept returning to it even though his superiors wanted his total concentration on something more pressing. Good coppers dreaded a case like Daphne Tolliver's. One they couldn't solve.

It had eaten away at Culverhouse for at least five years, keeping him awake at night. The very fact he'd arranged a reconstruction of the murder five years on proved that. It was true that reconstructions were well-suited to a TV programme such as Crimewatch. It made good television. Although the public swallowed the idea that they were a good thing, Freeman always thought it smacked of desperation. All avenues have been exhausted. Let's dress a WPC as the victim and see if anyone remembers seeing her. Gus wasn't a fan.

He noted one fresh item teased from the memories of the good townsfolk as a result of the broadcast. A birdwatcher saw Daphne with her dog chatting to another man twenty minutes before she died. However, there didn't appear to be any progress in identifying that person. The additional clue didn't form part of the reconstruction, so the man's memory wouldn't have been jogged. Even if he had watched the programme, he might not have come forward. There were a dozen reasons for that eventuality.

Nevertheless, accepting an eyewitness's opinion that the couple knew one another was naive. Therefore everything was alright between them. They may have looked to be chatting amicably, but one wrong word could have flicked a switch in the other man's brain. The graphic images of the victim suggested she suffered a sustained and vicious attack. Whoever she met in that clearing was hell-bent on stopping her from living to tell what was said or seen. Gus reckoned the identity of the unknown man was a line of enquiry worth pursuing.

Did his superiors need his old-style policing methods, or did the request come out of pity? Did they plan to occupy his mind with fruitless digging into age-old cases the best young brains failed to crack?

Darker clouds crept across the sky, and dusk wrapped a cold hand around his shoulder. It was time to tidy up, lock the shed and make his way home. A single malt with his name on it sat indoors, and enough time for a last review of the case notes.

He would sleep on it. The ACC gave him twenty-four hours to come to a decision. He needed every second.

Thursday, 29th March 2018

Gus Freeman slept late. He had reread through the thick folder and decided that the ACC was right. They needed to find the person responsible. Daphne Tolliver didn't have an enemy in the world until that evening. Gus was unconvinced by any suggestion in the newspaper article that a serial killer had struck in the area. His nose told him it was someone local and that Daphne was in the wrong place at the wrong time. Her killer had a secret they would do anything to protect. That narrowed the field.

The temperature struggled to reach double figures by lunchtime, and a stiff breeze helped the passing clouds scud across the sky. The rain was only hours away. The only consolation was the breeze that would usher the showers to the next county within the hour.

Gus considered what might happen if he accepted the ACC's offer this afternoon. Would they ask him to start work as early as next Monday? Did they already have his two officers and the graduate poised to join him? Surely, they couldn't have recruited people when he had given no sign that he was keen.

Did Geoff Mercer have someone else in the wings ready to grab the role if he refused it? That was more his style. No doubt he had a mate from the funny handshake brigade. He'd heard the rumours.

There was little doubt the police service was now far more inclusive and diverse. The Freemasons was an organisation for men, which was inconsistent with the values and reality of the modern police service. That has been the most significant factor in reducing the influence of the secret organisation to the margins in recent years.

Since Gus retired, the Police Federation passed new rules on how it ran itself. These new rules aimed to end the fact its vital senior officials were white and predominantly male.

The new regulations meant Freemasons leading to an old boys' network were much less likely in the future. That still didn't preclude Geoff Mercer from pulling a fast one and helping one of his brethren.

Their paths crossed over the years. Gus thought him to be a candidate for an OBE. But, no matter what case he supervised, the rest of his team put in the hard yards, and Mercer always managed to take the plaudits from the top brass. On one occasion, he'd tried it on with Gus when their teams ran a joint operation involving a gang of ram-raiders that terrorised half the county for several months.

"Excuse me, Geoff," he'd said, elbowing the Detective Inspector aside as the press rushed to interview them outside the Swindon County Court, "you can't expect to get the glory for other buggers' efforts."

The pompous ass had drifted away like a deflated balloon. A lot of water has flowed under the bridge since then. Mercer wouldn't have forgotten it, though, and others congratulated Gus for taking the chancer down a peg. That would have hurt him and possibly slowed his progress for a while.

Perhaps that was why the ACC was so quick to remind him Mercer was now a senior officer, and he needed to give him the respect his rank deserved. Geoff had indeed climbed further up the greasy pole than Gus ever managed. But, no doubt, he had help based on Gus's assessment of his capabilities.

Gus clung to the ACC's promise that the teams reporting to Mercer were free to run things as they saw fit. They suffered no interference from above. If Gus wrapped up a case or two in short order, Mercer wouldn't have an opportunity to get his own back. This afternoon promised to be fun.

The morning was slipping away from him. The Community Shop next to The Lamb could cater to his basic needs over the coming days. His freezers were well-stocked.

He wouldn't starve. Gus ran the hoover around the rooms and dusted where he thought it was needed most. He lifted the lid of the laundry basket. Not enough in there to warrant putting on a wash until the weekend.

He thought back to yesterday. He automatically threw on the same clothes again this morning. Well, on any typical day, he would potter in the garden or at the allotment. It wasn't a fashion parade. Staff in the local shop didn't bat an eyelid if he strolled in wearing his gardening clothes. They'd seen more bizarre sights. Mrs Ida Lubbock popped across the road for a pint of milk one morning in her nightie. It left nothing to the imagination. They kept a close eye on her at the care home if she got the urge to wander.

Gus stripped off his sweater, shirt and trousers. They were grubby, with a lingering odour of *Eau de Bonfire*.

"Sod it, I might as well do the lot," he muttered, and a pair of socks and his underwear joined the growing pile. "The question is, can I find something to wear?"

Tess bought most of his clothes. Gus wouldn't have chosen some of it, which explained why so much looked nearly new when he opened the wardrobe door. There seemed an awful lot of it. His suits were tucked away on the left-hand side. After he retired, he vowed never to wear one again except to a funeral. Little did he know.

The few items he enjoyed wearing were straight ahead. It made sense to have them readily available. Things like the pink shirt, the polo neck jumper and the mustard-coloured cardigan were as far from the centre as possible. He'd worn them at least once to avoid upsetting Tess's feelings. His hand hovered over the plain shirts and trousers, deciding which sweater to choose.

"Do I want to impress them?" he asked himself, "they wouldn't have thought much of my appearance yesterday."

Gus stood in his clean underwear and socks. It was time for a change. The pink shirt might look good with his navy blue suit. Tess had sent his suits to the dry-cleaners before storing them in zip-up garment bags. He found the trousers tight on the waist but remembered the extender button that offered a half-inch relaxation. Ah, joy of joys, he'd be able to sit without being cut in half. Where did Tess hide his ties? A rummage in a few drawers produced the navy blue he needed to complete the ensemble.

He ran a hand through his hair and risked inspecting the results in the full-length mirror inside Tess's wardrobe door. What would Vera the Vampire make of him in a suit? Was that what was behind this dressing-up malarkey?

"I thought we agreed that we didn't need complications?" he asked his reflection.

He couldn't go in stockinged feet. Did he still have a pair of proper shoes? Gus hunted through the bottom of his wardrobe and located a pair of lace-ups, black, size ten. He was suited and booted.

These shoes had been in the cupboard since Tess's funeral because he'd never needed anything smart. They were dusty and lacked any real shine. Gus couldn't remember whether he had any shoe polish in the house. He would never have thought to buy any.

"I've made enough of an effort for one day. Time to return to my inner rebel."

With that, he shone his shoes on the back of his trouser legs. That sorted that.

The drive into Devizes was more eventful than yesterday. The first heavy rain showers met him head-on as he passed the town's football ground on Nursteed Road. When he arrived at the junction to join the A361, the traffic was threading past a broken-down oil tanker opposite The Crammer.

A glance at his watch told him he'd make it with minutes to spare if he was as lucky at finding a parking space as yesterday. But his heart sank as soon as he pulled off the main road and looked through the trees at the available parking spaces. Not a gap to be seen.

Up ahead, a bright yellow sports car was reversing. It was an Alfa Romeo 4C Spider Convertible, no less. Gus had seen it yesterday and wondered which top brass officer was trying to recapture his youth. But, at least the numpty hadn't left the top down. There was nothing worse than driving in a sports car when your arse was in a puddle, so they told him. But, of course, he would never have fifty grand to splash out on, even a 2015 version of the big banana. So he had to take their word for it.

Gus waited for the car to leave enough room for him to pass and grab the vacant spot. Geoff Mercer would be tapping his watch and tutting now. Gus was impatient to get into the building. What did the numpty want now? Instead of driving towards the exit, the car stopped, and the driver's side window lowered with a movement as smooth as silk.

It wasn't a fifty-year-old boy racer, Gus realised. It was Vera, the Vampire. She wanted to speak to him.

Gus prayed his window would lower without sticking or dropping of its own volition. Just one of the innovative design extras Ford hadn't intended to release to an unsuspecting public.

"It might be a tight squeeze," she said breathlessly.

Vera had encouraged him to park in her space.

He knew he had a stupid grin on his face caused by her innocent remark. Gus straightened his tie in case Vera hadn't noticed the improvement in his appearance. He had to do something to distract her attention and get rid of the indecent image he enjoyed.

"You look very smart. Good luck this afternoon. Bye."

With that, Vera left. The Alfa was out of the car park and halfway into the town centre before Gus edged his ageing Ford Focus into her parking space.

A different young officer staffed the Reception desk today. Gus signed in, waved his Visitors Pass at him, and then bounded up the stairs two at a time. He was out of breath when he stood outside the ACC's door, but he gathered himself and knocked before entering. Truelove stood by the window again. Gus wondered whether he witnessed the exchange between him and Vera.

"Sorry, I'm a minute or two late, boss,"

"Mercer couldn't make it until a quarter past two, no rush," replied the ACC.

Gus Freeman sighed and sat. Typical.

"Mrs Jennings has the afternoon off today. Young Kassie will serve our refreshments this afternoon. With a K, if you please. Whatever happened to normal first names, Freeman, eh?"

Gus couldn't care less about how she spelled her name. All he could think of was Mrs Jennings.

Call yourself a copper? How did you not notice a bloody wedding ring? Of course, she'd be married. Nobody in their right mind would leave Vera on the shelf.

What a prize prune he must look in this suit and a pink shirt, dressed up like a dog's dinner.

CHAPTER 5

Somewhere in the background, Gus heard the door open and voices.

"Ah, you've arrived, Geoff. Let's get the formalities over with and get cracking."

The Superintendent's physical appearance hadn't altered over the years. He still resembled a balloon.

"Welcome back, Freeman," said Mercer.

Gus shook the small, sweaty hand that snaked out from the corpulent body. A memory of an image of one of the Mr Men entered his head. Not a great start.

"Thank you, Sir," Gus replied. No point in antagonising the bloke.

"I've explained how this Crime Review Team will function, Geoff. Freeman has the documentation required to get the ball rolling. When we met yesterday, we agreed that he could mull over the proposal overnight and inform us today whether he was happy to accept the consultancy role."

"What do you think of the set-up, Freeman?" asked Superintendent Mercer, "is it something you could manage? I appreciate you've been out of the loop for a while. Things have changed in the intervening period. Your operating procedures may need reassessment. The officers we've chosen to help you are experts in what is acceptable language and what's not."

"I believe I've always known what's what, Sir," replied Gus.

He cursed himself for the comment sounding abrupt.

The ACC had moved away from the window and sat in his executive chair. Mercer remained standing. The reason for this was apparent. If he had sat in the chair beside Truelove, it would be tricky to see the short-arse over the family photographs adorning the ACC's desk.

"Play nicely, you two," said the ACC, "I hope we can move on from the issues you had when you were both serving detectives. The victims involved in these cold cases deserve our very best attention. So let's consign the petty squabbling to the past."

"That's fine by me," said Gus, "I can see where you were coming from on this Tolliver case. Whoever was responsible needs catching."

"So, does this mean we have a green light to set up the team?" asked Truelove.

"It does," said Gus, "but there's the odd issue I need to resolve first. For instance, how much time will I need to commit?"

"A cold case is far different from an active investigation, Freeman. The way I see things, your team would work normal office hours, five days a week. If you felt you needed to step outside a basic nine to five, you clear the overtime with me first. We're running a tight ship."

"Superintendent Mercer will be your immediate superior, as I explained," said the ACC. "I suggest he shows you around the Hub later. You can see where a large percentage of your information will come from. This consultancy role will differ from your previous experience. Less stressful, I hope, but just as satisfying. In the old days, you both worked a hundred hours a week and had no idea when you would get home. When you ate a meal without the phone ringing…."

With that, the phone rang. The ACC answered.

"I thought I said to hold my calls, Kassie?"

The conversation was brief. When it ended, the ACC replaced the phone and stood.

"The Chief Constable and the Police and Crime Commissioner wish me to join them at once. The balloon's gone up somewhere."

He's stood just beside you, thought Gus.

"I'll get Kassie to bring through the refreshments. It may be a while. Geoff, I suggest you carry on with Freeman's list of issues. Once you resolve those, if everyone's happy, perhaps the team can become operational from Monday week. Is that achievable?"

Truelove stood by the door, waiting for a reply.

The two men still eyed one another with caution.

"Provided this list isn't too long, I believe we can make it happen," said Mercer, smiling at Gus for the first time. It was disconcerting.

The ACC left the door open. A chubby teenager wheeled a tea trolley into the room. Kassie Trotter was unlike any clerk Gus had seen when he was a serving officer. Kassie's right arm bore a full-sleeve tattoo from the shoulder to the wrist. The intricate design in a myriad of colours featured Japanese dragons and stylised flowers and foliage. Her sleeveless black vest made it easy to see it in all its glory. Her black jeans fitted where they touched. One side of her head was shaved, and the remaining mane of black hair was tinted electric blue at the tips.

"Do you want sugar?" she asked, a spoonful hovering over a china cup on the trolley.

Gus shook his head. Her eyebrows were thick and black. They seemed to be stencilled higher than nature intended. The girl looked permanently frightened. As Gus stared at her ear piercings, nose ring and labret, he thought it odd that *she* looked afraid.

It was he who was scared to death.

Geoff Mercer had got used to her appearance.

"Two sugars for me, Kassie, please,"

"Cutting down, are we?" asked Kassie.

Gus stifled a laugh.

"I've got cakes," the young girl continued, leaning forward to retrieve a plate from the lower tray of the trolley.

Gus noticed more tattoos. A small heart on the left, a bluebird on the right, as you looked at them. They disappeared when she stood upright.

"Baked them myself," she added proudly.

"It would be rude of me not to try one," said Gus.

"I was leaving the plate," said Kassie, "You always insist, don't you, Mr Mercer?"

Geoff Mercer went redder and redder. The balloon would burst in a minute.

"I'll come back in half an hour," said Kassie as she wheeled the trolley towards the door. "I want to see empty plates, okay?"

"That's us told," said Mercer as the door closed behind her.

"Things certainly have changed," said Gus.

"Kassie's heart's in the right place."

"I did notice."

Geoff Mercer smiled more naturally at that remark and brought his cup of tea and two cakes over to sit beside Gus.

"Look, we need to clear the air. I was a different person when we crossed swords all those years ago. Blind ambition made me behave in a way that I'm ashamed of now when I look back."

"Sometimes we need to block out things happening around us to achieve things that don't seem possible," said Gus.

"I reached a rank I never dreamed of, but I'm under no illusions. Detective Superintendent is as far up the greasy pole as I can climb."

It was evident from his slumped shoulders that it had been a tough pill to swallow.

"I've done plenty of reading in the past couple of years, trying to make sense of it," said Gus. "You were extremely ambitious, aiming to become Chief Constable. Nothing less would be good enough. To paraphrase Machiavelli, if you get to a position where you cannot climb higher, then all you have to look forward to is a fall from a great height. At least, that's the gist of it."

Mercer sipped at his tea but did not comment at first. Instead, he relaxed his shoulders and eased back in his chair.

"The austerity programme had begun when you retired. It never stops. Job cuts, increased workloads and stress levels for the remaining employees have led to a deterioration in mental health. Those of us in senior positions are not exempt. We're in situations daily where we feel we've let down the public. We feel we've let ourselves down. So it's no wonder some take that last drastic step. Suicides are on the increase."

"You must avoid blaming yourself for failing to grasp the ultimate prize, Geoff. That way lies madness. The job's not worth falling into the pit of despair and never climbing out of. Instead, listen to the voice of experience."

"I can't imagine what you've been through, Gus. Despite everything, I've clung to my wife and children. I didn't deserve to. I wouldn't blame Chris if she'd given it up as a bad job. On the few occasions I got home for any length of time, I behaved like a pillock. Then, the ACC told me how your wife died. That must have been an awful shock. An aneurysm, wasn't it?"

"It was, although I knew nothing about the condition or how it affected people until afterwards."

"How long had you been retired when it happened?"

"Six months."

"Shit. Could nothing have prevented it or managed it? It just seems so brutal."

Gus found himself agreeing with Mercer for the first time.

"A brain aneurysm occurs when a weak spot in the brain's arterial wall bulges and fills with blood. It can affect a person at any age. If it bursts, as in Tess's case, it's an emergency that can result in a stroke, brain damage and death without immediate treatment. Tess was home alone that day. I'd gone to Swindon to give evidence in an armed robbery case. I didn't return home until eleven o'clock. The verdict saw three villains sentenced to the maximum term allowed. It was a time to celebrate the system working as it should for a change. My joy was short-lived. When I fell out of the taxi and rocked through the front door, three sheets to the wind, I found her on the kitchen floor. Her hands were covered in flour. She had been preparing to do some baking."

"Sod's Law," said Mercer, "if cases didn't take so long to get to court, it would have been wrapped up months earlier. You would have been there to get her the help she needed."

"It wasn't relevant. I don't blame myself for not getting home by seven o'clock which was when I told Tess to expect me. We'd been married long enough for her to realise things cropped up that buggered up our schedules. If the case had ended earlier, I could have been on the allotment for several hours that day. Unless I'd been stood beside her when it burst at around eleven or noon, she was done for, regardless."

"I'm so sorry," said Geoff Mercer, "were there no symptoms beforehand?"

"Tess would tell people she'd never had a day's illness. She suffered from common colds most winters, as we all do, but that didn't count in her book. Tess had measles, chickenpox and mumps as a kid and had her appendix removed at fourteen. The doctors asked me if she'd had severe headaches, pain behind the eye, blurred or double vision, etc. I told them, yeah, if we'd had a night out and suffered a hangover the next day. I have no idea whether she had any of those symptoms in the weeks before she died and yet was sober as a judge. She never complained. I was adjusting to being retired, to the pace of village life and a new allotment. Tess dashed back and forth to the college in Salisbury, working split shifts. That week it was half-term, and she was at home. I'd worked on the armed robbery case, and my boss called to say they would need me there to give evidence. They wanted to make sure the bastards went down. No way I wanted to miss out."

"I don't blame you. We work hard to get the villains into a court to see them get what they deserve. We know the system's flawed, but it's what we have to use. I have high hopes for this Crime Review Team. You were always a better copper than me. No, don't argue...."

"I wasn't going to," laughed Gus.

"Not many murders are committed on our patch in a year, thank goodness. We don't have the serious crime statistics of our major cities, but when we fail to solve a high percentage of the few we have, that doesn't sit well with me. We need to do better. Blokes like you are needed to educate the younger detectives in reading people. They think everything can be solved by checking suspects' social media accounts or using HOLMES and its free text database, which allows users to ask unstructured questions and present the results in order of relevance."

"Easy for you to say," said Gus, "that stuff is all Greek to me."

"It's possible to combine the skills and experiences of crime investigators with the acquired knowledge of the system to identify new lines of enquiry. Those statistics can provide a list of the people most likely to commit a particular crime."

"Where is this outfit housed? Here at HQ?"

"Yes. Do you want that last cake? If not, I'll keep it for Ron."

"Later on, yeah, I remember. No, you're fine. I've already had more cake than I eat in a week."

"Let's walk over to the Hub, then. As for those other issues you wanted to raise before you officially agreed to start work, perhaps we could talk them through later over a pint?"

"The only question I had was over the suitability of the Old Police Station as our home base. Until I look around it, I won't be able to tell whether it will work."

"We're limited to where we can house you. Of course, money is a big factor, but I felt it important for this case, particularly for you, to be near the murder site. I know you. You'll immerse yourself in your surroundings, root under the surface and follow a line of inquiry Dominic Culverhouse missed."

Kassie Trotter looked up as they left the office together.

"The cakes were scrummy, Kassie," said Gus, "thank you."

"You're welcome."

The tattooed clerk levered her bulk off her precarious-looking perch on an office chair and trundled her trolley towards the ACC's office to retrieve the tea things. Gus Freeman idly wondered what lay ahead. Was this graduate going to be a sight to behold? The ACC had hinted that she was no shrinking violet.

Geoff Mercer swiped a card through the scanner to gain access to what was a restricted area. Gus wasn't a stranger to desktop computers. His superiors may have considered him a dinosaur when he retired, but even he had picked up a few basic skills. He had also negotiated his way around his smartphone without asking for Tess's help. However, the programs the technical staff within these walls dealt with were beyond him.

"This is what we call the Hub," said his guide. "These tech wizards compare cases seeking matches. Inactive files are sent for processing from central after two years. These guys can run a program to see whether the MO matches any other cases we already have on file. They find a similar MO and then check the physical evidence. It might be a car that was sighted. A partial number plate. They couldn't match a DNA sample with anything at the time, but now there's a new suspect to match it against."

Gus could tell Geoff Mercer was proud of the tricks they could pull here in this ultra-modern suite of offices. The place must have cost a fortune. The lighting, air-conditioning and ergonomically designed accessories perfectly complemented the array of screens, scanners and printers humming merrily in the background.

A glance at the pictures on the walls confirmed they featured prints of classic paintings by Van Gogh, Gaugin, and Rothko. At least, he assumed they were prints.

Naturally, there was an official record of the day this Hub opened. The usual suspects were there. Stop it, Gus told himself. They were dignitaries, not suspects — the Chief Constable. Well, the one before the incumbent. That bloke had left under a cloud. Gus spotted the Police and Crime Commissioner. The man who held the purse strings. He looked pleased with himself. They couldn't have exceeded the budget by too much. The Mayor was there also, judging by the chain of office he wore. Gus scanned the remaining faces but didn't see anyone he recognised.

"Where were you that day, Geoff?" he asked.

"Cheeky bugger. I'm there at the back, behind the local MP. The big wigs made sure they got their faces in prime position. Those occasions are for showing off. They aren't like the old days on the football terraces where the little ones were passed over the heads of the grown-ups to stand at the front."

Once the tour ended, they returned to the main building. Geoff Mercer had a team briefing to attend in ten minutes. Kassie confirmed the ACC was still otherwise engaged.

"Right then, Gus," said Geoff, "I'll let you get off home. About that drink? The Bear, next to the Corn Exchange, do you know it?"

"I've driven past it many times, but I've never been in there. What time?"

"Let's say at eight o'clock. Is that good for you?"

"Is the first round on expenses, Geoff?"

"Get off with you. See you later."

Geoff disappeared along a corridor towards offices at the rear. Gus mused that it wasn't all sweetness and light in the Superintendent's life. He didn't qualify for a room with a view.

Kassie Trotter called out as he made his way towards the top of the stairs.

"It's cream cakes, Monday, for the Chief Constable's birthday," she said, "they won't be home-made, though."

"I won't bother dropping by then, Kassie," said Gus.

Kassie gave him a big smile. Her eyebrows barely moved.

Later that evening, Gus drove into the Market Place, parked the Focus and walked across to the sixteenth-century Inn. The place reeked of history, and even on a Thursday evening, the main bar was busy. He stood inside the door for a second. Geoff Mercer was on the far side, beckoning him over. Gus threaded through the mix of guests and regulars to the small table near a window. He spotted a half-finished pint of bitter. Geoff pointed to two stools.

"Take your pick," he said, "I'll get another half to go with this 6X. I can't risk getting stopped. What can I get you?"

"A pint of cider, please," Gus replied.

While Geoff waited for the bar staff to notice him waiting for service, Gus looked around the bar. There was little chance he'd see anyone familiar. He tried to recall what the pubs were like near his proposed workplace. He wouldn't recognise anyone there either.

"There we go then," said Geoff, managing to make his way through the crowd without spilling a drop. "Good health."

"Cheers," said Gus.

"So, the Old Police Station? You have reservations about it being suitable?"

"I have security concerns, given the nature of the confidential paperwork that we'll be holding. But something else struck me too. I get the thinking behind us using the place as a base in the town, and I support that. However, as they decommissioned the station, is it even legal for us to take people into custody for questioning there? Do we possess an observation room? Could we hold an identity parade, for instance?

"That's taken care of, Gus. I can show you the layout on Monday morning if you wish. You no longer have the power of arrest, but the ID card authorises you to carry out everything you need. I imagine most of your interviews will take place in the home or the workplace. You'll take an officer with you at all times on those occasions. When you need to use the facilities you describe I've arranged for the new station on the outskirts of town to be at your disposal. It will only require a phone call. They'll accommodate you if you want an ID parade. You'll have the necessary recording equipment available in the interview suites. If you decide to go it alone in an interview, your DS will be in the observation room. You can request a senior officer to observe if you opt for a good cop or bad cop routine. Whatever we do has to be squeaky clean. Despite this being a no-brainer of an idea, getting the PCC to cough up the finances wasn't easy. Be aware; he's hovering in the wings to pounce if you mess up."

"Duly noted, Geoff."

"I take it you haven't been to either of the stations in the town?"

"Never had a reason."

"I knew Dominic Culverhouse, of course, who worked there at the time of Daphne Tolliver's murder. Another fine officer we lost to Avon & Somerset. Surely, you must have heard of one of his predecessors, Phil Hounsell?"

"Ken Truelove mentioned him briefly, but although his reputation made it further than Salisbury, he was another one I didn't get to work alongside. You've both given me background on him. Why?"

Geoff Mercer rang a stubby finger around his collar. Gus guessed he might not enjoy what he was going to tell him.

"Hounsell had a good team around him there. Then there was Terry Davis. He was a DS but a lazy sod. Everything was too much trouble. We were thankful when he took early retirement six years ago. He lives on the outskirts of Marbella now."

"Costa del Crime? That's the rumour."

"So, why is Terry Davis relevant?"

"His son Neil is one of your Detective Sergeants."

"Terrific."

"There's never been a whisper that Neil takes after his father. The lad is twenty-eight years old, recently married, and on a fast-track to higher things."

"Do you have any other surprises for me?"

"We've had to modify the offices at the Old Police Station to accommodate DS Alex Hardy. Alex joined the police after university, and his passion for motorbikes saw him train as a qualified pursuit officer. Twenty months ago, he was seriously injured in a high-speed crash while chasing a suspect. He is thirty-eight years old, single and in a wheelchair. He joins the Crime Review Team as part of his rehabilitation. Alex is adamant that he will eventually recover sufficiently to resume active duties. We have reservations, but he has had to be incredibly strong-willed even to make it this far. So who knows?"

"I imagine he will be permanently confined to our base, leaving Davis as the only DS able to accompany me on investigations. What shocking revelations will I learn about the graduate? Don't bother. I'll find out soon enough. You've given me enough things to worry over tonight."

Geoff drained the last of his drink. He patted Gus on the shoulder as he rose from his stool.

"I'll meet you at your new abode at nine on Monday morning," he said, "I promise you there's no cause for concern. Hardy and Davis are good coppers. They both understand how to use the digital support system at the Hub. They'll find out anything you need to support you in your face-to-face dealings with witnesses. Rely on them; rely on the system. That's why the resource is there. When you need a senior officer to make an arrest, call me or someone on the list that I'll send to you on Monday."

With that, Geoff left. Gus looked at his glass. Should I stay, or should I go? He caught sight of Geoff through a crowd of people. He had stopped to talk with someone. Best to follow his boss's example. He could drink at home. Although, after what he'd heard tonight, maybe he needed more than one. He finished the cider. It had certainly hit the spot. It was tempting, but he, too, eased his way past young and old customers until he reached the door into the hallway. Geoff was nowhere in sight.

"Drinking with the boss, were we?"

Gus half-turned and was pinned once again by those green eyes. Vera Jennings sat with three other women, and they were on a table by the window.

"A girls' night out, Mrs Jennings?" he asked.

"Something like that," she replied, "Mr Mercer tells me you accepted the consultancy position. That's good news."

"I'll be back in harness six miles up the road from Monday week," said Gus.

"I'm sure our paths will cross," she replied.

She rested her fingers on his arm.

"Call me, Vera," she said, "and sweet dreams."

As Vera Jennings rejoined her friends, Gus escaped to the car park. The woman made smart casual and white trainers look like the hottest outfit ever.

Gus drove back to Urchfont village. Whether there was much traffic on the road didn't register. He pulled into the driveway and parked the Focus. The roses Tess had nurtured as they climbed the trellis to the side of the bungalow seemed to turn their heads away from him.

Once indoors, he hunted through his record collection for something to suit his mood. Tonight he needed the blues. The Authorised Sister Rosetta Tharpe Collection would suffice. Some nights he listened to classical; on other nights, artists such as Armatrading, Dylan and Marley.

He owned an eclectic mix of albums. Music wasn't an ever-present thing with him. Immediately after Tess's death, he had listened to Gluck, Chopin, Mahler and Purcell. Brief spells of melancholy interspersed with long hours of silence.

A large glass of a full-bodied Malbec from South-West France sat on the table beside him as he let the music wash over him. Alex Hardy, Neil Davis and an unnamed feisty female. Were they ever going to bond into a capable team? Why had he agreed to return? As for Vera Jennings and the electricity he'd felt when she brushed his arm. What did that mean?

Gus stood up to make his way unsteadily to bed. His glass and the empty bottle teetered on the edge of the table and fell to the floor.

"Sweet dreams," he muttered, "if only."

CHAPTER 6

Friday, 30th March 2018

Gus climbed out of his bed at around nine o'clock. He had a sore head. That served him right. He made his way gingerly to the kitchen and filled the kettle. Coffee. Black. That was the first order of the day. Breakfast would come later.

The empty bottle and glass lay on the carpet by his chair. They suffered no real damage. It pays to empty these things before you knock them over. Gus left them where they landed. His head told him it couldn't face bending that far just yet.

Sister Rosetta Tharpe still sat on the turntable. Waiting in vain for the chance to prove she was the actual creator of rock and roll. Gus slid the album into the much-loved sleeve and returned it to a place of safety.

The coffee helped a little. The weather outside the window hadn't changed from yesterday. The forecast was changeable for the last week of the month. There was nothing to argue about on that score. Gus hoped he could get showered and dressed if he managed another coffee and maybe a slice of toast.

It was eleven before Gus felt ready to walk to the allotment. The breeze did its best to clear the cobwebs from his brain, and he managed some digging before noon. There was no sign of Frank North this morning, but Bert Penman was toiling away. Gus strolled across.

"Morning, Bert. How are things?"

"The sun and rain are arriving in equal amounts, and it's slowly getting warmer," Bert replied, continuing to fork over the straw he'd packed around his strawberry plants. "All things to encourage things to grow the way they should.

Fingers crossed we don't get another sharp frost again, though. You can never be too hasty, but we might be over the worst."

Bert leaned on his fork and stood to look at Gus.

"You have the world's troubles on your shoulders, if you don't mind me saying?"

Gus smiled. The older man didn't miss much.

"I had too much to drink last night, Bert. On top of that, I'm returning to work for a while."

"Couldn't stay away from a job you loved, is that it?"

"There's a case they want me to have another crack at solving. It's been nagging away at Wiltshire Police for years. A fresh pair of eyes."

"You don't have to tell me anything about it. That's fine. I understand. But, if you want me to keep an eye on things, say the word. I'm here every blessed day. It's no hardship."

"It would take a load off my mind, Bert. I'll be free at weekends. I might fit in an occasional evening. Unfortunately, experience tells me I'll not have the spare time I have now."

"I'm not just offering out of the goodness of my heart, lad. If your patch is covered in weeds because it ain't getting tended to, they'll spread over to mine. I can't be doing with that."

Gus put an arm around the older man's shoulder.

"Thanks, my friend. Just don't overdo things. I need to learn more from you yet."

"You won't learn much from that Frank North, that's for sure," laughed Bert. "He potters about here for as long as he does because his wife won't let him smoke anywhere near the house. Half of everything he puts in the ground would stay there and rot because he's never sure when it will come out."

"Why don't you tell him?" asked Gus.

"What, and miss a few free helpings to get me through the winter? My pension isn't that great."

"You crafty devil. Your secret's safe with me. I'll let you get on, Bert," said Gus, "I'm driving into town to get supplies. I don't know when I'll get the chance again."

Gus left Bert Penman chuckling to himself. Poor old Frank North. Thoughts of the ex-con and his spindly cigarettes reminded Gus of the suspicious goings-on he mentioned on the hillside behind Cambrai Terrace. As he walked towards the gateway from the allotments, he studied the tree line that sparked Frank's interest.

If he had his Dad's binoculars, it would help. They were in the loft if memory served. His father had joined up at eighteen in 1944. He was stationed in Germany until 1949, then came out of the Army, and he and Mum got married the following year. The repatriated pair of binoculars had belonged to a German officer. They were a high-class piece of engineering.

"Hang on, what was that?" Gus stopped in his tracks.

He couldn't be a hundred per cent sure from this distance, but he thought he'd seen a trail of smoke from behind that stand of osier willows.

It might be an idea to get those binoculars from the loft. That smoke might merit a closer look.

Sunday, 1st April 2018

Gus had caught up with his household chores yesterday. He filled the fridge and the freezers with supplies. While in town, Gus had a haircut. Since being retired, he wasn't concerned about curling over his collar or blowing in the wind. Those things seemed important when in uniform, even when he was a detective.

Tess mentioned from time to time in the weeks before she died that a haircut was overdue. Just a gentle reminder. Gus always thought it rich, remembering what a hassle it could be for her to get a brush through that mane.

He checked his appearance in the mirror when he got home just after lunch and considered himself ready to meet head-on whatever challenges came next. Later that afternoon, a visit to the loft uncovered the vintage Dienstglas 6X30 military binoculars. The glasses were of top quality.

Gus popped to the allotments in the evening, where he found Frank North sitting by his shed, deep in thought, cigarette shielded from the breeze by his hand.

"Busy, Frank?" he asked.

"I've done what I came here to do," he replied, "and now I'm planning my next job."

"I'll forget I heard you say that, Frank."

"No, Mr Freeman, honest to God, I swear I didn't mean that sort of job. I wondered whether to try spring onions and green beans this year instead of leeks. I don't get them to survive as others do around here."

Gus wondered whether Bert would enjoy spring onions and green beans as much as the leeks. He waved the binoculars at Frank. "Brought these along," he said.

"Have you seen something then, Mr Freeman?"

"Not sure, but I thought I saw smoke up there on Friday."

"That's it," said Frank, getting excited. "As I said, that bloke's growing osier willows but doing nothing with them. They're growing unchecked. The chap who had that land before him ran a little market garden. He'd grow early varieties of vegetables and fruit, then sell to small, independent shops in Devizes, Pewsey, Market Lavington and Upavon. He became successful, outgrew the place and moved. He had a shed built when he needed a store for the rotavators, seed drills, and tools he bought. Only breeze blocks and a tin roof at the start. As the business grew, he had a roof put on and added mains water and electricity to the shed."

"The smoke could mean someone's living up there and lighting fires."

"They've never asked for planning permission if they are," said Frank.

"These glasses can stay in the shed from now on, and I'll watch for any suspicious activity," said Gus. "There might be a legitimate explanation for the smoke if that's what I saw. If it looks dodgy, I'll pass the details on to my colleagues."

"Your former colleagues, you mean, Mr Freeman," grinned Frank.

Gus didn't need to explain his consultancy job. Bert Penman wouldn't say a word to Frank. He couldn't afford to now. Gus knew the secret of the missing vegetables.

"Do me a favour, Frank. Don't go nosing around up there. If they're up to no good, it could be dangerous. It's best to leave these things to the professionals."

"Understood, Mr Freeman."

Monday, 2nd April 2018

Gus decided to dispense with the suit this morning for his trip to the Old Police Station. He didn't know what condition the first floor of the building would be in if it had been unoccupied for a while. Moreover, if his suit got dirty, it needed dry-cleaning before the following Monday when he officially took up his new post.

Gus donned a clean pale blue shirt, navy blue slacks and a leather jacket. It took five minutes to get ready but a further five minutes to find a comb. After that, he would have to stop running his fingers through it and make do. Gus convinced himself he wasn't trying to impress anyone. Witnesses responded better to smartly attired policemen, despite TV cop shows like 'Columbo' and Peter Falk.

He'd missed this feeling. He was itching to join in the banter and form friendships with the new people. Not just at the Old Police Station but the new custody suite on the outskirts of town and the Devizes HQ.

Gus even looked forward to meeting Geoff Mercer this morning. He wouldn't have believed that a few years back. He looked at his watch. Shit. He had to get a wiggle on if he wanted to make it on time. He buffed the tops of his shoes on the back of his slacks and slammed the door behind him.

Everything had a purpose and meaning again.

Gus joined a steady stream of traffic on the main road out of town and enjoyed the view as he motored towards his destination. Devizes's elevated position meant that he saw the urban sprawl of the market town in the valley as he came closer. He wasn't sure which was which, but the Westbourne and Greenwood estates were visible. One on either side, like two lungs. The main drag through the centre retained evidence of several light industrial companies, but the heavy industry disappeared a generation ago.

A sign on a roundabout pointed to where the custody suite now sat. Gus checked the mileage indicator. Within two miles, he had parked next to the Old Police Station. Not too far to travel to access those added facilities. They'd cope.

Superintendent Mercer was waiting at the rear of the building. Geoff's uniform looked pristine, as it had when they met in the ACC's office.

"Good morning," said Mercer.

"So, this is where we'll be working?"

"Yes, but let's go in the old front door on the High Street first."

There used to be a comfortable similarity to a police station front office as far as Gus was concerned. He must have visited dozens of these old Victorian examples. The horrors they knocked up in the Sixties were an abomination by comparison. However, when they stepped inside what they now affectionately called the Old Police Station, the sight that greeted him made his heart sink.

Gus tried to imagine what the old place looked like before the transformation. He could still see the mouldings on the walls and the lights suspended from the ceiling appeared original. Besides that, the ground floor was partitioned into two units by the modern half-glass, half-panel screens. A corridor between the two appeared to lead to a communal rest area in what had been the back offices and cells.

"I know what you're thinking," said Mercer, "the Food Bank operates out of the unit on the left. The Cancer Charity occupies the right-hand section. What you see here is typical. Loads of activity, people in and out eight hours a day, six days a week. Let's go upstairs."

Geoff led Gus back out to the High Street.

"The Crown is over the road, and The Ring O'Bells is further along on this side. Those are your two closest pubs."

"I like a man who has his priorities right."

Gus had noticed the car park at the rear of the building was in better order than the interior they had just left. The newly installed lift to the first floor was roomy and quiet. However, when the doors opened, Gus realised that the ACC had fooled him. The suspended ceiling and sympathetic lighting highlighted a modern open-plan office layout with all the bells and whistles he and his team would need.

"Not what I expected," he admitted.

"The ACC and I wanted to be certain you wouldn't turn us down."

"What else do I need to do before next Monday? Will I meet the team members beforehand? What's the plan?"

"Straight in at the deep end. Nine o'clock on Monday. Your Sergeants are used to working with fresh faces. Teams don't stay together for as long as they did in the old days. Today will be the first day's work for Lydia, the graduate. Ease her in gently. Perhaps, you can arrange a visit to The Crown after work on your first day. The food's not bad. You can use the occasion for a spot of team bonding. While I remember, the ACC asked me to hand you your ID card."

Gus looked at the authorisation he needed to carry in the future. He recalled the full police badge and his well-earned

'Detective Inspector' he carried until three years ago. This card looked like a bus pass. It bore his picture and 'Wiltshire Police Civilian Consultant' written alongside it.

"We'll take a quick spin around the amenities, and then I must get cracking. I need to be at HQ, and I can't depend on every traffic light turning green. That ID card doesn't look much, but it is programmed to give you access to this place. I'll arrange for the others to receive their swipe cards before Monday."

The Superintendent continued the brief tour of the first floor. Gus saw they had catered for everything needed to accommodate DS Hardy and the mysterious Lydia. Things were improving. Maybe this job wouldn't be such a hardship.

The two men returned to the ground floor.

"You know where I am if you need to update me before next Monday," said Gus. "I'll keep you abreast of everything we are doing as we progress our enquiries."

Geoff Mercer nodded, and this time the handshake was far more friendly.

"Glad we cleared the air and managed that drink together last week," he said.

"The Bear's a busy pub. I noticed that the ACC's PA, Mrs Jennings, was there. She stopped me for a word as I left."

"I saw her too. Vera was with her friends in that club they formed. We call them the last of the few."

Geoff laughed so much at his comment that Gus wondered what he'd missed.

"Sorry, Gus. It's not funny. I told you how fortunate I was my marriage survived despite my being a workaholic. A few years ago, a group of not-so-lucky ladies started socialising. Some were divorced, and others separated. One by one, they've found new partners. There is only a handful left now."

"So, Vera's divorced?" Gus tried not to sound too interested.

"They've been separated for a time—only weeks before Vera loses the ball and chain. Vera had the afternoon off to visit the solicitor on Thursday. It may be cruel, but young Kassie Trotter started calling them the few. She said the FEW stood for - the frustrated ex-wives club."

Gus tried to make light of what he had learned.

"There's more to Kassie Trotter than meets the eye," he said, "a mischievous sense of humour wasn't what I expected. It beats me why Mrs Jennings is still not spoken for, though. Or her other three friends. They were more than presentable."

"Sorry, spoken for and more than presentable? Those are rather dated expressions, aren't they?"

"They were in common usage when I was a young man, Geoff. No doubt I would find I'm out of touch if I looked for someone to grow old with now Tess has gone. The language would be the least of my worries. Nobody meets at the youth club or the local hop anymore. I bumped into Tess in a pub, and the rest was history. It's all done on an app these days, so they tell me. I would have no chance."

"Chris and I met in a pub too. It was a different generation, that's true. Youngsters today do things differently. Blimey, I can remember not getting past first base for weeks. Today, most of them have done the business before choosing which subjects they're studying for GCSE in Year Nine."

"All our yesterdays. I'll let you get back to Devizes. I think I'll wander around the town, then check out The Crown when it opens. For research, to see what's on the menu ahead of next week's bonding session."

Geoff got in his car, but before he closed the door, he called out.

"Gus, what the kids get up to today is irrelevant. The last of the FEW are almost as old as us. I cannot find out, but I guess they will talk roughly the same language as you did back then. If you're thinking of returning to the game, that is."

"I'm not sure I'm ready to move on. I feel as if it would be betraying Tess's memory."

"Tess wouldn't have wanted you to be miserable. So why not dip your toe in the water, and take someone to dinner, no strings? Also, look for someone to be a 'plus one' at a Police Federation function. There's bound to be a lady just looking for company."

With that, Geoff Mercer gave Gus a friendly wave and was gone. Gus stood alone in the car park and took stock. They had a decent base from which to work. By all accounts, both of the serving officers in his new team had a good track record. Davis might have a father with a murky past, but young Neil started with a clean slate.

Hardy sounded like a terrific prospect who had suffered a life-changing accident. Gus had met people with a range of disabilities in his career. For the first time, he would have the opportunity to work with one. It might pose problems, but they had to overcome them. The team owed it to DS Hardy. He'd moved mountains to get to this stage in his recovery. Alex Hardy was fiercely independent. Driving himself to and from work was not going to be an issue.

Then there was Lydia. Twenty-five. What had the ACC told him? Gus couldn't remember Truelove giving her full name or any description. There must be a note on her background somewhere. Was it at home in that thinner file he had read? Perhaps he overlooked it. Because when he started reading it, he was erring on the side of giving a return to work a miss.

The Daphne Tolliver murder file got him seething with anger that such a selfless soul died so callously.

Gus strolled from Church Street onto High Street. There were still dozens of people visiting one of the two units inside the old station. He passed the Imperial Dragon Chinese Restaurant and noted it was takeaway only on

Mondays, which was a shame. If he decided to take Geoff up on his team bonding suggestion, a meal in a place like that would have been a possibility.

As he drew closer to Market Square, he saw the typical indications that the traditional shopping pattern was breathing its last. Nevertheless, a handful of independent retailers were still fighting to stay alive. He recognised the name of Patel's newsagents. Daphne Tolliver had advertised in there when she searched for part-time work.

A pet food store, a unisex hairdresser, and a camera shop surrounded estate agents and building societies. The banks in town had closed. Instead, two national clothing outlets had a branch on the Square for women, both with massive discounts plastered across the windows. It looked so depressing.

Gus knew that supermarkets, DIY stores, and the usual array of fast-food outlets on the outskirts of town that out-of-town shopping centres featured. They were all alike. You could be anywhere. Drive two hundred yards further on, and you reach the light industrial estate with a family pub owned by a chain with similar establishments up and down the country. They served the same ice-cold drinks, offered identical menus and did it at a price the independents couldn't hope to match. Town centres might have to bring back public hangings as entertainment to get anyone to visit them in the future.

"Well, this won't cheer me up," thought Gus as he rounded the corner and left Market Square. Then he saw the light at the end of the dark tunnel. Two restaurants. One on either side of the road. An Indian and an Italian. Not a risqué joke. Both restaurants offered fine dining by candlelight and takeout. Happy days if he found a 'plus one' for a night out.

Twenty minutes, and he'd covered the most significant elements of the heart of the town. The Crown was open. Could it be opening time already? Gus checked his watch and then spotted a sign that said they served breakfast until noon and a choice of a wide variety of coffees. He had to wait until eleven o'clock if he wanted something more substantial. He ordered a black coffee, which proved almost as challenging to rustle up for the sixteen-year-old behind the counter as the exotic varieties on offer.

Gus studied their menus for lunchtime snacks and evening meals. They served the usual steaks, pies, fish, and a vegetarian option on the starter and main course. So it might do for a team bonding evening, but not for anything more important.

Hark at me, he thought, making plans without even considering who might be interested. So, Vera Jennings was soon to be divorced? So what? If Kassie was correct, and she wasn't seeing anyone, it could mean she'd sworn off blokes altogether because of how her old man had treated her. Or, she was only interested in snaring a bloke with enough money to provide her with a pricier car.

Of course, if he decided to leap into the unknown with someone, he could always cook at home. Either his home-grown vegetables would melt their heart, or the limited number of recipes he'd mastered would persuade them he needed rescuing. What a nightmare.

Gus finished his coffee and walked to his car. A steady drive back to Devizes, and he could take a quick look at those folders again this afternoon while he checked on his allotment. He had to make the most of the free time he had left.

After preparing a quick snack to take with him to the allotment, he flicked through the items the ACC had given him that related to HR matters. He had completed the forms that needed signing and sending to London Road. Ah, there it was, a brief CV for Lydia Logan Barre.

The Forensic Psychology graduate was born in Edinburgh in 1993. Her mother was Scottish, and her father was Nigerian. Lydia was adopted at birth by a white couple living in Dundee. Despite racial bullying at school, she had a happy childhood and remained close to her adoptive parents.

When she left school, she had ambitions to become an actress. She attended part-time classes at the Royal Scottish Academy of Music and Drama in Glasgow. Lydia then switched focus to the MSc at Glasgow Caledonian University, which she completed last summer. Gus knew this was her first full-time job, but it impressed him that Lydia must have supported herself while she did her part-time stint in Glasgow. He wondered what prompted the switch to such a markedly different discipline. That was something to monitor.

The brief notes told him as much as he needed before meeting Lydia on Monday. The picture showed a striking young woman with coffee-coloured skin and a head of hair resembling reddish-brown curly corkscrews. That girl was going to make an impact wherever she went. If he'd ever seen anyone more confident in her skin, he couldn't remember them.

Gus took his packed lunch and the murder file with him as he left the house. Time to catch up on revision. He soon sat in his comfortable chair and became lost in the tragic events of 2008.

Reviewing the murder file revealed the difference between dealing with a fresh corpse and a cold case. When the police discovered a body, the information to gather still lay there somewhere. If you found the correct information, you could find the killer.

In a cold case, other detectives had done the work for you. The autopsy report and the crime scene photographs were to hand, and you had a catalogue of forensic results. Witnesses had been visited and interviewed, sometimes more than once.

He knew the members of Daphne's family still around would never get over her violent death. Any suspects they had identified in 2008, even if soon exonerated, would still be tarred with the experience for the rest of their days. Neighbours would cross the road to avoid speaking to them. The stench of suspicion never left them.

The information within the covers of the folder would soon spread across the Crime Review Team office. Four pairs of eyes would examine every piece.

Gus thought of them as pieces of a jigsaw. He couldn't wait to put those pieces together.

CHAPTER 7

Monday, 9th April 2018

The alarm should have woken him at seven o'clock. Gus had been awake for at least an hour, thinking of what lay ahead. He silenced the annoying ring and sat up in bed. The job itself didn't faze him. It was the prospect of meeting new people on whom he had no background.

Gus needed to establish a hierarchy that would benefit the team's overall effectiveness. He needed to avoid bashing Hardy and Davis over the head with his former rank and obvious age and experience. They would understand the processes. Unless they made an absolute Horlicks of something, he needed to sit back and let them demonstrate the level of their skills.

Lydia was the unknown quantity. Yet, the merit pass she received last summer marked her as a more than capable student. They would be lucky to hold on to her for long. Once she had work experience, she would quickly move into a more senior position. The ACC relied on Gus to mould her into a shooting star. A gleaming success of his burgeoning back-door recruiting programme helped alleviate the wounds the austerity cuts had delivered.

Whatever he did, he must resist limiting Lydia's involvement, so she felt her contribution was irrelevant. She had a fiery character, according to Truelove. He had to balance out his three staff members' input. Alex Hardy's mobility issues needed delicate handling. It made for an interesting morning. Solving the cold case might prove simpler than keeping them happy.

His suit hadn't suffered too much in its recent outing. He just had to decide which colour shirt to wear. Gus shoved the pink one further along the rail. It wasn't a day for pushing the boat out. Today called for one of his several white, button-down collar shirts and a brightly coloured tie to lift the mood. His hair refused to play ball despite the comb being exactly where he had left it. Wetting his fingertips to stick the offending spikes to his scalp didn't help. It still looked like he'd stuck his fingers in a light socket.

Gus sighed, left the bungalow with his folders, and set off in his trusty Focus.

He found a critical alteration to the car park when he arrived a few minutes before half-past eight. Either the ACC or Geoff Mercer had exercised their rights as the landlord to refresh the white lines. Also, there were now four spaces next to the rear wall of the building with a 'Private Parking - Police Personnel Only' notice on display.

The remaining spaces were available for business staff on the ground floor. Whether the fresh layout balanced out the four parking bays the CRT had grabbed, Gus couldn't tell. It wouldn't affect deliveries. There were already spaces on the High Street with dropping-off restrictions in front of the Old Police Station.

Once upstairs in the office, he chose a desk and sat in the chair. He could keep tabs on his three staff members from here, and the whiteboards and other displays would be visible. Which of the three remaining desks would be best for DS Hardy? Was it an idea to split the two guys up and fit Lydia between them? Decisions. Decisions.

Gus had twenty-five minutes before anyone else would arrive. He started loading the boards with photographs from the crime scene. A map of the surrounding area. A breakdown of the victim's family, neighbours, work colleagues, employers and anyone who could have come into contact with her.

"Do you need a hand with that, Sir?"

Gus turned to see who had exited the lift. A young man late twenties, six feet tall. He wasn't overweight, maybe thirteen or fourteen stones, but he looked trustworthy rather than athletic. His brown hair was cut short, and his brown eyes looked bright and alert. He was smartly dressed, and it wasn't hard to work out which team member had arrived early to impress his new boss.

"You must be Neil Davis," said Gus, shaking the newcomer's hand. "Good to meet you. No need for the 'Sir'. I'm a mere consultant now. My DI rank is ancient history. I know it will take you time to adjust from something that's second nature. I prefer 'guv' when we're in the office or out in the field. I'm happy for you to call me Gus in social surroundings."

"Right you are, S... guv. Are these the contents of the murder file? We were told the first case under review was the 2008 Tolliver murder, but it was before my time. I read the press reports on the case over the weekend. It was a brutal business."

"Good to see you're not coming in cold," said Gus, "The ACC and Superintendent Mercer have chosen well. The Tolliver case must be solved. The downside is that if we fail miserably, I'll be back tending to my allotment, and you'll get transferred pronto."

"We had better not fail then, guv," said Neil, sorting through items Gus had spread out on the desk and quickly finding what he wanted. The boards started to take shape. The CRT office was coming alive.

Gus looked at the wall clock. Ten minutes to nine. The other two should soon be on their way upstairs.

"Let's take a break from this, Neil and test out the amenities. I saw a Gaggia in the restroom when Superintendent Mercer showed me around last Monday. I won't make it a habit, but a decent cup of coffee will be a good ice-breaker when the others get here. We can chat about the day ahead while the four of us rate the cuppa against the swill most station machines cough up."

"Blimey, guv, a Gaggia is a step up from what we usually get. This office must have cost a packet to fit out."

They didn't hear the lift descend to the ground floor over the sounds of the coffee maker. A minute later, Gus and Neil heard voices in the office and returned from the restroom.

The young woman was instantly recognisable from the photo Gus had seen in the folder. So, this was Lydia Logan Barre. Gus learned she was medium height, possibly a size twelve, based on a comparison to Tess at the same age. Although side-lined in the past year and a half, her artistic background still influenced her dress style. Her skirt was black leather, but her blouse was a riot of blue, orange and green. Gus heard the sharp intake of breath as the dramatic effect made an impact on Neil Davis. Her hairstyle hadn't changed.

Lydia's companion in the lightweight wheelchair looked pale and drawn. Alex Hardy looked every one of his thirty-eight years. Yet Gus sensed a steely determination in the way he held himself. Alex's record showed him a shade under six feet tall, twelve and a half stone, with fair hair and blue eyes. Before his accident, he played several sports, visited the gym weekly, and enjoyed mixing with friends. He would have been Gus's ideal number two in this team two years ago. Life can be cruel.

"Welcome, you two," said Gus, "I'm Freeman, and this is DS Davis. Guv and Neil from now on."

As Gus shook hands with Lydia and Alex, Neil stood by the restroom door.

"Coffee's ready," he said, "how do you take yours?"

"Black with one sugar," said Lydia.

"White, no sugar," replied Alex, manoeuvring his wheelchair next to the nearest desk.

"Let me get that chair," said Lydia, nudging the office chair away towards the outside wall.

"Right, that's two of us sorted," said Gus. "why don't you sit in the middle, Lydia? Neil can occupy the desk nearest to the restroom. Although nobody should assume that means he's on permanent refreshments duty. No matter how good this coffee he's brewed tastes."

"We've got a Gaggia," said Neil.

"We've got soft-close toilet seats too," said Gus, "but let's not waste any more time. I've checked out The Crown around the corner on High Street. I suggest we get better acquainted there over a drink and a bite to eat later. Is that OK, or are any of you required urgently elsewhere?"

"I can ring Melody to tell her I won't be home until around eight o'clock," said Neil.

Alex and Lydia didn't raise any objections.

"Right," said Gus, "let's go through why we're here and what will occupy our time in the coming days."

Gus gave them a brief resume of his former career and the facts surrounding the murder. Alex Hardy had done his homework, like Neil Davis, which made progress easier. However, it was clear the murder scene images shocked Lydia. Gus caught her staring at them throughout his opening comments. She needed someone to hold her hand and guide her through these first few days.

Gus finished his introductory spiel and summed up: -

"As with every unsolved murder in the county, this case remains open. While there are currently no new lines of enquiry, I believe the key to solving it lies in the community shown on the map. Loyalties and relationships change as time passes. People may be more willing to tell us what they know. They may share suspicions today that they had at the time but hid from us. Ten years is a long time to carry a terrible burden."

"What about the reconstruction they did five years ago?" asked Alex, "that threw up a possible new line of enquiry, didn't it?"

"They never found the running man or woman," said Neil, "and never identified the bloke on Battersby Lane."

"DI Culverhouse, who investigated this murder the first time around, was under pressure to get a result," Gus cautioned. "His superiors would have moved him on quickly. New crimes crop up every day. It's easy with hindsight to criticise. We might ignore his methodology this time around, and we may not. It could prevent us from identifying the killer. It didn't do *him* any good. He would have done things differently if he had had unlimited time and resources. Maybe, he would have found his killer by following his chosen path. Our advantage is that we can set our own pace and think outside the box. We can trace different witnesses. We won't get another case handed us until we finish this one."

"Where do you want us to start, guv," asked Alex Hardy.

"We can't do anything to improve our knowledge of the murder scene or the forensic results gleaned. In ten years, the whole area will have altered. I may visit the park to give myself a feel for the distances involved relative to the location where we know people they did identify were. We will keep the victim's photographs in a prominent position here as a permanent reminder of why we're doing this. Daphne's family deserve to see justice done. Alex, I'd like you to get me a list of the witnesses interviewed and confirm their current whereabouts.

"Understood, guv," said Alex. Gus sensed him less than enthused about being automatically selected for mundane desk duty. It wasn't the most exciting job. He'll have to get used to it, Gus thought. It will be something trivial that gives us the most significant breakthrough.

"Neil," he continued, "can you contact the Hub, please? Five years ago, the reconstruction uncovered an eyewitness. A birdwatcher saw Daphne on Battersby Lane talking to a man. Did he describe that man at the time? If not, find his name and sit him with an artist to create a photo. Culverhouse believed the man was known to Mrs Tolliver and, therefore, no danger to her. Ask the Hub to age the image. Then we can appeal to the public for help in identifying him. A picture of what he might look like now compared to how he looked in 2008 might prove beneficial. We need to discover whether he was a threat or not."

"Will do, guv," replied Neil, "the sketch of the running person done at the time of the murder wasn't much use, was it? Is there any point in asking the Hub to age that as well? They might find a similar description from the recent past where the guy if it was a guy, committed another assault or murder."

Gus pondered this for a second.

"Make sure you get the Battersby Lane image first. The young runner Holly Dean saw would be between twenty-five and thirty years old now. You're right, it could be useful for reference, but I'm not looking outside the community for our killer. We'll need the Hub to do more valuable searches in the days ahead. Tagging Daphne to a list of crimes committed by a serial killer would be a waste of their resources."

Neil began to hunt through the murder file to find the identity of the bird watcher.

"Is there something you can give me to do, guv," asked Lydia. She sat on her hands, with her legs swinging back and forth.

"You can clear away these coffee things," said Gus, grinning at her. "Then, put on your thinking cap. In a town of this size, how many eighteen to twenty-four-year-olds were there in 2008?"

"You don't plan on interviewing all of them, surely, guv," asked Neil.

"Hardly, but use your head, Neil. What was the upside of the sketchy physical description of the person high-tailing it towards the park.?"

"They were young and agile," said Neil, "and wearing a blue anorak."

"Find the bird watcher, then keep digging in that file, and if the witness's description isn't detailed enough, find Holly Dean. Ask her to tell us how tall this person was."

"Height, weight and any disability will reduce the number of potential suspects by a big percentage," said Lydia.

"This could be a rare occasion when average height and weight might be helpful. If only to narrow the field."

"They won't all still live in town," said Alex.

"If you've got five minutes after compiling that list, you can pitch in and help Lydia. Two heads are better than one."

"Bloody Norah," yelled Neil.

"Paper cut?" asked Gus.

"No. Worse than that. The bird watcher was Percy the Pervert."

"Is he known to us?"

"Not half, Percy Pickering, to give him his proper name, has been on our radar for a few years. So, ten years ago, he was on Lowden Hill, supposedly bird-watching. As Percy swept the horizon for our feathered friends, he spotted two people and a dog on Battersby Lane. It took five years before he came forward with that information. Two years ago, I arrested him. It was a good week for me. We received a phone call from a concerned member of the public. They told us Gavin Shaw, a twenty-four-year-old Lothario, was knocking seven bells out of a gentleman on his doorstep on the Greenwood Estate. I drove around with a DC to find Percy Pickering with his face battered and covered in blood. Shaw was screaming at him, calling him a pervert. Pickering didn't defend himself. Shaw claimed Percy's bird-watching was a front. As technology had moved on, he could zoom in on the real object of his search and photograph it. Shaw said Pickering visited Lowden Hill to spy on young courting couples and swingers who frequented the wooded areas. It had been a favourite haunt for horizontal refreshment for decades."

"How do you know?" asked Alex, "did you go there?"

Neil's face reddened.

"As it happens, at fifteen or sixteen, I did on several occasions. Once I got my driving licence, I stopped sneaking around there. Anyway, I left my Detective Constable with Shaw and helped Pickering indoors. He needed medical attention, but I thought I should at least try to stop the bleeding until the ambulance arrived. He was nervous as hell. It made me think there was truth in what Shaw claimed. I stayed with Pickering while my DC took Shaw to the station. I texted him to flag up my concerns, and twenty minutes later, he returned with our Inspector. Percy caved before the DI could admit she hadn't got a warrant to search the house. He took us upstairs, and we found he had a library of still photos of couples going at it, young girls on their knees...."

"I think we get the picture, Neil," said Gus, "Lydia doesn't need to hear the blow-by-blow details. Shit. Forget I said that."

"Pickering must have been at it for years. You haven't heard the best bit yet. The DI found a series of pictures featuring Gavin Shaw. He liked them young. When she turned up an image of her fifteen-year-old daughter sitting astride Shaw with a look of absolute joy, I had to stop her from killing him there and then. Anyhow, the result was that Pickering and Shaw got banged up. Sadly, the DI's daughter was too a few months later."

"Well, at least we know where to find Pickering to describe our unidentified man," said Gus.

He was pleased with how things had gone so far. They had lowered several barriers. The banter started to flow. He watched as his team continued with the tasks he had set them. Hardy, Davis and Logan Barre. The name conjured up a firm of accountants, perhaps, or solicitors?

Neil Davis could leave at some point. Lydia would be fast-tracked whether he liked it or not. Gus decided it had to be to a bloke called Willis if she married.

Yes, Freeman, Hardy and Willis. Now, that would be something.

Gus turned to his computer. The Land Registry would be the place to search for who owned the land where the osier willows grew. Time to do some research.

Alex Hardy had identified ten names Gus Freeman would want to re-interview.

Megan and Mick Morris were now both in their mid-seventies. They still lived in the same house as they did in 2008. He would suggest Gus talk with them together.

Their three children - John, Kathy and Fiona were in their forties.

John had been married to Stephanie, and they had two kids, but the marriage ended in divorce three years ago. John lived alone in Filton, Bristol. Stephanie had remarried and lived in Brisbane, Australia, with her new partner Amelia.

Kathy married Jack Nicholls. One daughter. They still lived on the Westbourne Estate.

Fiona married Emilio Mazzaro. Four children. They had moved to Newbury, Berkshire, six years ago.

Isaac Crompton - General Manager at the Manor House. In his early seventies. Dementia.

Joyce Pemberton-Smythe - Fifty-eight. Married to Leonard Pemberton-Smythe. Sixty. He became Junior Minister in the Home Office in 2010, promoted to Secretary of State for Justice in 2015. Hotly tipped as next Home Secretary. Two boys. Both are working at the family vineyards in France.

To that list, he added people who might provide information that hadn't previously surfaced: -

Holly Wells, nee Dean, married Danny Wells. Two boys. The family lived in Chippenham.

Carl Brightwell was twenty-seven. Another one it's easy to locate. Currently residing at HMP Bristol. Formerly Horfield Prison. Grievous Bodily Harm with intent. Section 20. Out next year. He was terrorising the public at

McDonald's, so he wasn't the killer, but that didn't mean he didn't know someone with a grudge against the old lady.

Neil's revelation meant they must interview Percy Pickering. He wasn't the killer, but he might provide more details on the unidentified man.

There were the Managers and staff at the Charity Shops. Ditto at the Post Office. Names would be a chore to uncover. Most of the Charity Shop staff were volunteers. Quite a few of Daphne's work colleagues could have died in the interim.

Mr Patel from the Newsagents in Market Square. Daphne's neighbours. Either of those could have had means, motive and opportunity.

They could talk to Wally's mates if they wanted a group of outsiders. Did one of them have a dark secret? Good luck finding them now.

However, their best bet undoubtedly would be to identify the two missing people: - The young person in the blue anorak and the man on Battersby Lane. They were vital in solving this case.

Alex looked across to where Lydia sat, deep in concentration. Perhaps he should offer to help. He expertly negotiated the waste bin and covered the distance between the desks in a flash. A deft spin brought him alongside the attractive young woman.

"How far have you got?" he asked.

"To find the overall figures won't be difficult. Breaking them down the way the boss wants will be much harder. We can get names, ages, gender, working or in full-time education, and whether they're registered as disabled. Outside of that, it's hopeless."

"We may have to get inventive to ascertain height and weight. Use social media."

"Not everyone is on social media, and they don't always post pictures of themselves. Hundreds of people only photograph their pets to share online. We need to reduce the numbers first; otherwise, that would take months. Is there a way for the Hub to help?"

"I'll send the comprehensive list of names and ask them to highlight people with a criminal record. The killer may have committed other offences."

"If nothing else, it will allow me to talk to someone outside this room. This kind of job is so boring. I want to be making progress."

"Welcome to the real world of work," said Alex, "same old shit, every day."

On the other side of the office, Gus Freeman had uncovered the name of the person who now owned the land behind Cambrai Terrace.

Bernard Jennings.

That had to be Vera's estranged husband. Why did he need an isolated piece of land? What did the smoke signify? What was behind the alterations to the storage shed? Gus wondered who to ask. He picked up the phone and dialled HQ. Reception put him through to her extension.

"Kassie?"

"Who's that?"

"Mr Freeman. Can we talk?"

"Had enough already?"

"No, nothing like that. Look, what are you doing later tonight?"

"I might not be that sort of girl."

"Nothing like that either. I need information, and I don't want it blabbed about when you're at work. Do you understand?"

"My lips are sealed."

"Good to know. Can I pick you up around ten? I'll be driving a Ford Focus."

"The old one, yeah, I saw it in the car park. I live in Worton. Why don't you pick me up outside the old Rose and Crown? Nobody will be around. Only I watch 'Game of Thrones' on Monday, so I can't leave home until ten."

"The village pub? I'll find it. Thanks for this, Kassie. I promise not to keep you from your bed for too long."

"I'll have showered and put on my 'Game of Thrones' onesie by then, anyway. So I'll throw on a fleece to pop out to see you. I can jump straight into bed as soon as I get indoors again."

"Your parents won't mind you leaving home so late?"

Kassie laughed.

"Call yourself a detective? They haven't cared where I was since I hit sixteen. I live on my own. I rent a room from a mate."

Gus ended the call. All he could hope was Kassie Trotter was right and that there would be nobody in the village at that time of night. But, if they saw a young girl dressed as a wildling getting into a car with a man his age, they would have sleepless nights.

When his boss was available, Neil Davis had a question.

"Won't we be running a murder book on this case, guv?" he asked.

"Not in its typical format. For Lydia's benefit, the murder book includes the paper trail of a murder investigation, from the first report until the arrest of a suspect. The thick folder we've been utilising contained the crime scene photographs and sketches, autopsy and forensic reports, transcripts of investigators' notes and witness interviews."

"What will we use instead?" asked Alex.

"As I said, we'll have to accept most of what is in this folder as gospel. I suggest we start a central file we can access, which documents every task we do. So, those tasks I assigned today, the progress you've made, and what's left to do will go in that file at the end of each day. That avoids repetition and things getting missed altogether."

"Do you want me to organise that, guv?"

"Please, Alex. On this case, you'll be our anchor man. We can reassess that situation in the future."

Alex knew what that meant. He was stuck in this office as long as he sat in this chair. Lydia sensed him tense a little when Gus made that comment. He had helped her this afternoon. Maybe she should offer to help him keep the central file updated.

"Let's give it another couple of hours," said Gus, "then we'll call it a day and spend an hour or two relaxing in The Crown."

After five, they added their contributions to what Alex had dubbed The Freeman File. The team travelled in the lift together and headed onto High Street. The Crown was quiet at that time of day. Gus bought the first round of drinks, and then after suggesting they split the food costs four ways, he surprised them by settling the bill on his way back from a trip to the Gents. Geoff Mercer had been right. The food was good enough. It wasn't fine dining, but it represented good pub grub. The banter flowed, and Neil had plenty of stories to keep them amused. Gus noticed none of them featured his father, Terry.

Alex was the quiet one. Gus had wondered whether he would open up about his accident and where things stood regarding his recovery. Maybe that would come later when he felt more comfortable with his role within the team.

Lydia proved much louder after two drinks. She spotted an advert for a karaoke night on Friday and tried to persuade Alex to come with her. Gus felt keen to be somewhere with her, but not a karaoke night.

Because the bar was half-empty, their team drew more attention than it deserved. Perhaps it was unusual to see suits in the Crown. Neil suggested they call it quits.

"We don't want to push it, guv," he said "you get a few rough buggers in later in the evening. They won't take kindly to their boozer teeming with coppers."

Lydia thought it wasn't only coppers the Crown's clientele weren't happy to see. She kept that thought to herself. It wasn't a new experience for her. Anyway, how many police officers wheeled themselves into a bar?

"We're only four office-workers unwinding after a busy day," she shrugged, "they'll get over it."

Gus agreed. They wouldn't make a habit of using this place. Its reputation outweighed its convenience.

"A moving target and all that," he said, "let's get off home. We can try out another watering hole another evening."

When they gathered on the pavement outside, Gus told them not to be late in the morning and headed for the car park.

He had a meeting in Worton. Wherever the hell that was.

His sat nav didn't let him down. Although he muted the annoying female voice, it reminded him of a schoolmistress who hadn't been his biggest fan.

Gus slowed as he neared the village and crawled towards where he was picking up Kassie. The road ahead was dark. Street lighting was sparse in these parts. Villagers were tucked up indoors at this time of night. There wasn't the hustle and bustle of a busy town with the late-night shops and fast-food outlets opening.

He spotted Kassie. Hard to miss her. The scarlet fleece was like a beacon on a landing strip. She hopped inside the Focus.

"Floor it, Freeman. Let's move."

"I thought we'd sit here and chat."

"Oh, OK. What do you need to know?"

"What can you tell me about Bernard Jennings?"

"Monty, d'you mean? Nobody calls him Bernie. His Mum regretted it as soon as he started school. Kids dashed to their front door, rang the bell, shouted 'Bernie in?' and ran off, pissing themselves with laughter."

A dim memory of eating at a Berni Inn with Tess in their courting days flashed through Gus's brain.

"Why are you asking about Monty? He's married to Vera. Well, for a little while longer, he is. Fancy her, do you?"

"I'm not interested in Vera. It's Bernie I'm interested in."

"Never."

"Not in that way. Look, let's start again. Why is he called Monty?"

"That soldier from the war. Montgomery. He was a Bernard, wasn't he? There you go. The name started it, plus he was a little sod who strutted about thinking he was something special. So, everyone started calling Bernie Jennings, Monty."

"He and Vera make an unlikely couple. What does he do for a living?"

"If you came from around here, you would know. Vera's family have farmed in the area for centuries. They're mega-rich. She was the only daughter. Her brothers have taken over from their father now. Monty has never worked for anyone all his life. As soon as he left school, he started buying and selling. You know, he's one of those...."

Gus looked at Kassie.

Even in the gloomy interior of the car, he could see her mouthing the four-syllable word, practising it, so it came out right the first time.

"entrepreneurs," she said, enunciating the word slowly. "He's got a lot of properties, which he buys to let out. Monty's had more get-rich schemes than you've had hot dinners. Some do okay; most fail miserably. Monty chased after Vera for months, and he wore her down. He's a few years older than her. I reckon he's older than you but doesn't look after himself like you."

"You're too kind."

"I need to go to Specsavers. Anyhow, Vera's Dad saw through Monty before they got married. He tied her money up so Monty couldn't get his hands on it and chuck it down the drain as he did with his own."

"No wonder she can afford to drive that Alfa Romeo," said Gus.

"Monty has been a prince and a pauper at least three times since they got hitched. The rumour is he's in trouble again. Their kids have grown up and left home, so Vera came to her senses and decided she'd had enough. Can't say I blame her."

"Well, that's told me enough about Bernard 'Monty' Jennings for now. I'd better let you get off home to bed. How did you end up out here in the sticks, Kassie?"

"I know," she sighed, "I ought to be in the bright lights of a big city, didn't I? I tried it when I left home and crawled back eighteen months later. I sofa-surfed between school friends until they got fed up. Then I slept rough for eight weeks. Those were the longest eight weeks of my life. I was days away from having to start selling my parts. Mr Truelove helped me get back on my feet. He's a born-again something or other, and he caught sight of me in his headlights one night on his way home. The ACC and his wife took me in. He found people to help me and promised me a job if I got myself together and stuck to it. Heart of gold, that man. Never wanted anything in return."

The ACC had always been a good copper. Gus was learning that he was a bloody good bloke into the bargain. He'd kept that side of his life under wraps. Gus had never heard a whisper.

Kassie saw Gus staring at her.

"Penny for them," she said.

"Don't thump me, but I'm glad you stuck to it. You scared me at first, but now I could get to like you."

"Don't go soft on me," she said, leaning across and kissing him on the cheek. She got out of the car. "It was my cakes that were the clincher, wasn't it, Mr Freeman? Go on, admit it."

"Get inside in the warm, young lady. Sweet dreams."

He watched her waddle the short distance to a gateway. Once she disappeared and Gus heard a door slamming, he turned the car around and drove home to Urchfont. Monty Jennings was someone who made fortunes and lost them. What might his next get-rich-quick scheme be if he was on his uppers after the squeeze on the economy in recent years?

Maybe, something illegal. It was time to call in reinforcements.

CHAPTER 8

Tuesday, 10th April 2018

"This number of potential interviewees is daunting," said Gus as he scanned the names Alex Hardy had provided.

"We're pulling together a list of those living in the town, or just outside, with a criminal record," said Alex. "Lydia is waiting on the Hub for the answer."

"Where is she this morning?" asked Gus.

"I had a call from her late last night, guv," said Alex, "she forgot she had a dentist's appointment at nine. We'll see her before ten o'clock."

"You don't waste any time," said Neil, "does this mean she persuaded you to try the karaoke?"

"She thought it made sense for us to have each other's numbers to keep in touch. You and the boss left sharpish last night. Lydia walked to the car park with me."

"I should have thought of that yesterday," said Gus, "it's only three years since I retired, and whether you believe it or not, we had phones back then."

He added his mobile and landline details to one of the whiteboards.

"The ACC reminded me when he persuaded me to return to this consultancy role that I couldn't charge around the county alone. So every interview will be done by two of us. We'll start with Daphne's sister and her husband."

"Shall I call them, guv, to let them know you're coming?"

"No, Alex. I don't want to give them time to get a story together. Not that the sister had anything to do with the murder. Mick Morris is an unknown quantity. Those two will give me a better feel for Daphne's character and the family dynamic. The words in the original file tell it one way; often as not, the truth is a little different. By the way, even though the list was humongous, it isn't complete by any means. Don't forget her part-time cleaning job at primary school."

"Sorry, guv, it was an hour a day in term time after the kids had left. So I didn't think it relevant."

"It wouldn't be the first time they found a teacher doing something they shouldn't," said Neil.

"It's a lower priority, just as many others outside the top ten you've highlighted. We'll bear it in mind. Especially if a name crops up from the Hub showing someone who worked at the school now has a record. Right, where do the Morris's live, Alex?"

"No change from where they said they were on the day of Daphne's murder, guv."

"Let's go, Neil. You can drive."

They descended in the lift, and as they edged out of the car park, Neil spotted Lydia's bright red Mini turning into Church Street.

"Even the car's a bit in your face, guv, isn't it?"

"I thought that yesterday when we were in the pub. We'll need to persuade Lydia to tone it down. She will be meeting members of the public soon. The deaths in the cases we'll be reviewing occurred years back. The emotion won't be as raw, but the last thing they'll need will be Lydia standing on their doorstep wearing the colours of the rainbow. Please leave it to me. Diplomacy is my middle name."

"Have you ever lived anywhere like this, guv," said Neil as they entered the Greenwood Estate. A sprawling expanse of social housing built at the end of the Fifties.

"No, thank God," said Gus.

"These roads closest to the main drag were originally covered in prefabs. Churchill's answer to the housing shortage after WWII. They designed the timber-framed units to last a decade. In many towns, they still stood fifty years later. The asbestos panels hadn't been recognised as a problem when first mooted. Materials were in short supply, and the whole thrust of the Housing Plan was to get as many houses built in the shortest time possible. The cost was a factor, as always. Despite the shortcomings, people who lived in them loved them. As the population increased, with refugees from Europe coming over first, then more from the Commonwealth countries, they added more and more places to house them. This lot we're passing now had that concrete cancer. It cost millions to refurbish them during the Eighties."

"Was the Westbourne started at the same time?"

"Within five years. Both estates have their quirks; this side has Avenues, Gardens and Ways, while the Westbourne has Crescents, Groves and Closes. Town planners had it so much easier in the early twentieth century; Street, Road and Lane covered everything."

"Number 30? That's the one we want. The car's on the drive. Let's see what they've got to say for themselves."

The front door opened before the two officers had got halfway up the short concrete path between two well-kept patches of lawn.

"Have you found the bastard?"

"Mr Morris?" said Gus, holding his card up for the old man to see. "My name's Freeman, a consultant with Wiltshire Police. My colleague is DS Davis. May we come in?"

"What's happened?"

The white-haired lady who had spoken hovered behind the older man. The couple stepped back as Gus and Neil moved into the hallway.

"Let's shut the door on this fresh breeze and sit, shall we?" said Neil.

Once inside the front room, Gus could see theirs was a simple life. The furniture layout showed a large part of their day centred on the television. Every spare inch on the mantlepiece, window-sill and Welsh dresser contained ornaments and photo frames. Mick and Megan's family surrounded them like a comfort blanket. The gas fire burned, and the room was stifling.

Mick remained standing. Megan perched on the edge of her chair. Her hands in her lap wringing the life out of a white handkerchief dotted with blue flowers.

"There's no need to read anything into our being here this morning," said Gus. He and Neil sat side by side on the sofa under the front window. Not an enormous sofa. It was cosy.

"Please, Mr Morris, have a seat."

Mick Morris reluctantly sat in the chair next to Megan. She grabbed his arm.

"We wanted to inform you that my Crime Review Team is revisiting Daphne's case. No murder case closes until we've found the person or persons responsible."

"Not a day goes by when I don't think of her," said Megan.

"I know, love," said Mick. He turned to look at the two police officers.

"Megan and I were meeting Daphne on Sunday lunchtime. Things would have been different if we'd driven across to see her on Saturday instead of just ringing her."

"Daphne took Bobby for walks in several places," said Megan. "Nobody could have known where she planned to go that night. Not for definite. It couldn't have been deliberate. Mr Freeman, you said your name was, did you?"

"Yes, Freeman. I was a Detective Inspector in Salisbury before I retired. My role is as a consultant now. Can you tell us which routes she might have taken? I don't recall seeing that in the information we received. Maybe she saw someone in the woods she associated with somewhere else completely. Could you remind me where you both were that evening?"

"Mick and I were both at home watching the telly. We told the other Inspector that at the time. The uniformed police were on our doorstep just after 'Casualty' finished."

Why don't we make a cuppa, Mrs Morris?" said Neil. He took the old lady through to the kitchen.

"You didn't pop out for any reason, Mr Morris?"

"Hardly ever go out without Megan these days. We go everywhere together."

"Would you know the routes Daphne took when she walked Bobby?

"She could have cut across the fields from Battersby Lane and got home in half the time. Megan told me she was going on a long walk that night because Bobby hadn't been out all day. Now and again, she'd walk into town and back. In the winter, they used a short walk along Braemar Terrace. Then Bobby decided how long they hung around in the cold."

Gus made a note of the alternative routes. He also noted that Mick knew the intended change in routine. Did he tell someone?

"What about Saturday afternoon or early evening? Did you have any visitors?"

"Our son, John, dropped by for half an hour with the grandchildren. Other than that, we didn't go out. I never spoke to anybody apart from Megan until the policewoman told me about Daphne's attack at a quarter past nine."

The door from the kitchen opened, and Neil came through with Megan. Neil carried four cups of tea and Rich Tea biscuits on a tray. Megan still had the wet handkerchief.

"What did your son do that weekend, Mr Morris? Do you know?"

"What he always did. Spent time with the kids to make up for not seeing them in the week because of work."

"To get away from her, more like," said Megan.

"That would be Stephanie. Is that correct?"

Megan Morris nodded.

"Never see our grandchildren now," said Mick.

Megan sobbed into her handkerchief.

"How long ago did your son's marriage end?"

"The final decree was three years ago," said Mick. "It was over before that. She started seeing someone else."

"Another woman? Is that right? Were you aware of problems in the marriage when your sister died, Mrs Morris?"

"We realised things had changed. They didn't visit here as a family. If we called around to theirs, she wouldn't be as welcoming as when they first got together."

"When do you think things began to change?"

"About a year before Daphne was murdered. Stephanie had started going to the gym; to get her figure back after the babies. That's when that woman got her claws into her."

Neil's notebook lay on the table next to his cup and saucer. Mick's version of Daphne's dog walk routes matched what Megan had told Neil. He knew his DS would use the time wisely in the kitchen when the couple were apart. Gus added a note to his memos. Had John sought comfort elsewhere because he learned his wife was playing away?

It seemed John could have had a motive for killing his aunt. If he *didn't* know that Daphne planned to be in Lowden Woods and she found him with someone else. On the other hand, Stephanie could have had a motive if she had been with a female in the woods. Maybe Holly *had* seen a young woman running away.

Everything had reached a dead-end back in 2008.

Fresh possibilities were starting to appear. Gus continued to probe.

"Did you mention in passing where Daphne was going, Mr Morris?

"Can't remember saying anything. I could have done, I suppose."

"Did John go straight home from here on that Saturday afternoon?"

"He took the kids to the cinema. Then they got fish and chips and went home later."

"Was Stephanie home?"

Megan and Mick Morris looked at one another. They looked uncertain.

"I don't think we ever spoke about it, Mr Freeman. John would have walked in the door at about half-eight and got the kids off to bed. When we rang him after the police arrived, he came straight around. He told us Steph had stayed at home with the kids."

"Well, thanks for that. It's been handy. We may be back with more follow-up questions. Be assured; we will do our best to find the person who killed Daphne."

Gus and Neil stood up and prepared to leave.

"That's what Culverhouse promised ten years ago."

"I accept that, Mr Morris," said Gus, "but we've got more tools in our box these days. It's far harder for the killer to avoid capture. Our man or woman probably thinks they've got away with it. But, if they relax for one second, they'll slip up, and we'll pounce. This team has never failed to crack a case."

The two officers left the old couple on their doorstep, smiling.

"That cheered them up, guv."

"We do our best, Neil."

"A bit naughty, not telling them we haven't solved one yet either."

"We learned a lot there. Whether any of it is important, I don't know. But, if we keep unearthing little nuggets hidden from view ten years ago, it's only a matter of time before we learn which is the vital clue we need."

"Back to the office, guv?"

"Not yet. Alex left a message on my mobile. It came through while you were in the kitchen. He's arranged an interview with Carl Brightwell. We're off to Bristol."

"Why not call Alex back and get him to arrange for us to meet up with John Morris in Filton? Either at work or home. We can kill two birds with one stone."

"Good thinking. I'll call Alex anyway. He can tell us what progress he's made with Lydia today."

"A gentleman doesn't tell, guv."

"Just drive, Neil."

They left HMP Bristol at one o'clock. Carl Brightwell had offered very little of any use. He had no suggestions for the identity of the person in the woods. The original file said he had been a moody teenager with a chip on both shoulders. They had just left a twenty-seven-year-old dimwit destined to spend the rest of his life in and out of prison.

"Carl's alibi is rock-solid, guv."

"I lost count of the times he answered, 'no comment'. Where did he pick up the Bronx accent? I don't recall him ever spending any time Stateside."

"Brightwell's a muppet, guv. He thinks he's a hard man. Over half his mates with him on the night of the murder are in the nick. The others are either hooked on drugs or dead. He'll commit another crime within a month when he comes out next year. He won't know anybody on the outside. All his friends are where we left him, back in Horfield."

"A depressing thought, isn't it? What do we know of John Morris? Is he at home or work?"

"John's home this afternoon. He should be out of bed. Mick Morris's son works night shifts in a warehouse in Filton."

"What's the latest from the office, Neil?"

"We now have a list of those people in the area with a criminal record. So far, Alex hasn't matched a name to someone from our list of most likely candidates. Gavin Shaw had a record as a juvenile for an affray charge. No surprise, given his short fuse."

"Hold it, Gavin Shaw was twenty-four when you arrested him, right? He was sixteen in 2008. Shaw could be our youngster in the woods. He's known to use his fists when provoked. He might not have registered on Culverhouse's radar, but he laid into Percy Pickering, didn't he? If Daphne Tolliver caught him at it in the woods, he could well have lashed out and killed her."

"Gavin moves back onto the list of persons of interest, guv."

"Blimey, we're here already. It was only a five-minute drive from the prison. We may catch John Morris having his breakfast."

"Do you still call it breakfast when you work nights and get up in the early afternoon?"

"What else should you call the first meal of the day?"

"Eighty-six, eighty-eight and ninety. Here we are. The place looks a mess, guv. The garden is a tip; that car hasn't been through a car wash in months. Look at the large oil slick underneath."

"Neil, his wife buggered off to Oz with another woman and took his kids with her. Do you honestly expect to roll up and see a semi-detached house out of Ideal Homes?"

"Perhaps, not."

They could hear the TV blaring away inside as they approached the door. Neil rang the bell twice. Knocked hard on the glazed window and, as a last resort, yelled through the letterbox,

"Come on, Mr Morris. We know you're there. Open the door. It's the police."

A bleary-eyed man in his mid-forties dragged open the door. It might have moved more freely if he'd bothered to pick up the many flyers, complimentary newspapers and legitimate mail collected on the mat.

"What do you want?"

"John Morris? Wiltshire Police. I'm DS Hardy, and this is former DI, Mr Freeman. We're from the Crime Review Team, taking a fresh look into your aunt's murder."

"You got ID?"

The two officers held their cards in front of Morris's face. Whether they registered was hard to tell.

"Is this going to take long? I need to get ready for work."

"Unless you've suddenly switched shifts, or the chance of overtime has turned up since we talked to your employer, I'd say you've got six hours to spare. We won't be that long."

Morris gave Gus a long stare. Gus could almost hear the cogs working away inside his brain.

"Now, I don't want to stand on your doorstep shouting, so let's get indoors, and you can turn off that TV."

"If you give us the right answers, we can be out of your hair in no time," said Neil, stepping forward. Morris moved more quickly than when he answered the door.

The inside of the house wasn't any better than the outside.

John Morris flopped onto a leather settee covered with a woollen rug. He did not attempt to clear the empty lager cans, fast-food cartons and overflowing ashtrays from the seat and arms of the only other chair in the room.

If Neil had to sum up Morris's design style, he'd call it basic brutal.

"We're re-interviewing each of the members of your aunt's family," said Gus, "can you tell us your whereabouts on the afternoon of her death?"

"I took the kids into town. We spent an hour looking in shop windows. I treated them to a milkshake in a café. Then we called on Mum and Dad."

"Did you stay long?" asked Gus.

"I don't know. Thirty minutes? An hour, maybe? It couldn't have been long. I took the kids to the cinema later."

"What did you watch?" asked Neil.

"Daddy Day Camp. It had been out a while, but new films used to take ages to reach us in the sticks. These days you can watch them five minutes after release. If your kids are still in the country."

"What did you do afterwards?" asked Neil.

"The usual for a Saturday night. Fish and chip supper. We arrived home at half-past eight. Dad called with the news before Match of the Day started."

"Was your ex-wife at home when you got back?" asked Gus.

"Yeah, lounging on the sofa. I doubt my ex-wife had moved since we left the house. Lazy cow."

"I think that covers everything," said Gus, turning to leave.

Neil had stood beside him throughout the conversation. There was nowhere they wished to sit. When they reached the door, Neil stopped.

"What did you and your Dad chat about while you visited them in the afternoon?"

"I can't remember."

"Did it strike you as odd that your Aunt Daphne was considering walking through Lowden Woods that evening?" asked Gus.

"I had no idea that was where she was going. I can't remember either of them mentioning it. The kids dominated the conversation with their grandparents. That's what we did most Saturday afternoons back then. Now I sit in the pub and get pissed."

Gus and Neil left him in his pit of sorrow.

"That was a nice Columbo moment back there," said Gus.

"Thanks. John will never get over his wife leaving, will he?"

"We don't know the whole story, Neil. As coppers, we appreciate how many marriages break down. What's the usual reason? The unsocial hours we work. The wife's at home with the children. She has to cope with the illnesses, the tantrums, and the non-appearance of Dad at the school nativity. The list is endless. John worked all hours, Monday to Friday. At the weekend, he overcompensated for his time with the kids. I wonder if he ever took the wife out on a Sunday. Just the two of them. I doubt it. A small thing like that could have saved their marriage."

"Stephanie Morris found someone who told her she was beautiful. If he bucked his ideas up, he could find someone.

Will his kids ever visit while he's living like that? Never in a million years."

"We can't do it for him. He's going to want to change the way he lives for himself. He's not our man, though, Neil. The timelines don't work. I thought there was a possible motive, but if he *was* seeing someone else, it wasn't on that Saturday night."

"Another one crossed off our list."

"Back to the office, Neil. We can spend two more hours nagging away at the Morris family members. Move the pieces around the board. Try to make connections."

Once they returned to the Old Police Station, Alex Hardy gave them a rundown of the tasks they had handled in their absence.

"This is all in the Freeman File, guv, for us to keep abreast of our progress,"

"Or lack of it," said Lydia.

"I'm sorry, guv. We've corroborated the statements supplied by Stephanie Morris, as she was, plus Megan and Mick's daughters, Kathy and Fiona and their husbands, Jack and Emilio. They were where they said they were from the afternoon until the following morning."

"It is what it is," said Gus, "they couldn't all have done it. We're not talking Murder on the Orient Express.'

"We've removed Carl Brightwell and John Morris from the list, too," said Neil.

"Can you take us through the information supplied by the Hub, Lydia?" Gus asked.

"They delved into the 2001 Census data and determined there were thirteen hundred and forty men and women between the ages of eighteen and twenty-four living in the area we highlighted. There would have been a degree of movement in the intervening seven years. We're waiting for a more useful physical description of the youthful person seen in the woods. Once we get that description, we can reduce that list to a more manageable number. The results can't be conclusive, but if one of the names is known to us, it brings them into our number of most likely suspects."

"When you say known to us, that includes names on the large list of potential suspects that Alex compiled, plus those with criminal records."

"Yes, guv, sorry. I meant those we have begun investigating, plus those that a criminal record suggests we should study closely."

"Phew!" said Neil, "it's complicated, isn't it?"

"That's because we haven't talked to Holly and Percy yet," said Gus.

"They're our best bet for a breakthrough on the runner's description," said Alex.

"Gavin Shaw has difficult questions to answer if our updated description puts him in the frame," said Neil.

"I think we'll swap team members tomorrow. Lydia, you can come with me to interview Holly Wells and Percy Pickering."

"What do you want us two to prioritise while you're away, guv," asked Neil.

"Getting that list reduced in size. Use the Hub's resources if you can find the right questions to ask. The ACC and Geoff Mercer will be on my back if we don't fully use their shiny new toy. That's for tomorrow. Right now, it's coffee time. Your turn, I reckon, Lydia."

Gus watched her make her way to the restroom. As the door closed behind her, he turned to his two sergeants.

"There's a method in my logic, guys. Lydia's presence can help put Holly Wells at ease. She was a sensitive body based on the file. As for Percy the Pervert, well...."

"She will go mad if she finds out, guv,"

"All's fair in love and war, Neil. I won't ask her to wear a revealing top or stockings and provocatively cross her legs. Her mere presence can help distract him. I want him to tell me something he doesn't want to admit he knows."

"You need that conversation with her, guv," said Neil.

"Did I miss something?" asked Alex.

There was an awkward silence as Lydia returned with the coffees.

"Alex, can you arrange those meetings for tomorrow? I don't mind which order they're in, but nothing earlier than eleven o'clock. We'll meet here at nine, Lydia. Come dressed for a walk in the woods. I want to visit the murder site. We're missing something. I need inspiration."

Alex wondered why Neil was grinning. He would ask him in the morning.

"I hope you find it, guv, every stone we've turned over so far has just given us more trouble rather than less."

"*Trouble is the common denominator of living. It is the great equaliser,*" Gus replied.

"That's deep, guv," said Neil.

"Soren Kierkegaard," said Gus.

"Who did he play for, guv? It wasn't for any of the top six clubs in the Premiership. I would have heard of him. Was it Palace or Charlton when they had a brief spell in the limelight? He's like that, Eric Cantona, isn't he? The seagulls following the trawler, and that."

Gus groaned and shook his head in resignation. The youth of today.

"Kierkegaard was a philosopher, Neil," laughed Lydia.

"Oh, right. Well, my old English teacher told me that one new fact every day was the high road to success. I've learned something new today."

The rest of the afternoon saw Alex and Lydia searching social media to gather relevant physical descriptions for anyone they hadn't already eliminated from their listings. Neil and Gus keyed their versions of the day's witness interviews into the Freeman File.

When he drove home that evening, Gus wondered how long before he heard from Geoff Mercer. He'd relayed his concerns over what was happening on the land above Cambrai Terrace before leaving for work this morning. It might be something of nothing, but Geoff would call before long. Only two days into the review or not. The clock was ticking. The top brass would be itching for the team to make progress.

Wednesday, 11th April 2018

"Good morning, guv,"

Lydia arrived on time. She was wearing the ubiquitous Barbour jacket, dark trousers and knee-high boots. She strode across from her Mini to meet him as he stepped out of his car.

"Are we going straight there, or are we going up to the office first?"

"I need to check Alex received confirmation of our meeting times later today. Once I know we're okay with those, we'll walk the route Daphne Tolliver took. It's a nice day for it."

They travelled up in the lift to find Alex and Neil were already at work.

"Morning, lads. What news, Alex?"

"Mrs Wells is confirmed for eleven o'clock. I've left her Chippenham address on the card on your desk. Pickering resides at HMP Leyhill. You can be there in forty minutes via the M4."

"That's near Wotton-under-Edge, isn't it?" asked Neil.

"That's right. Category D for Delightful," said Alex.

"We'll leave you two to crack on, and Lydia and I will see you this afternoon," said Gus.

"Good hunting, guv," said Neil.

When they reached the car park again, Gus nodded towards his car.

"We'll use my car to get out to Braemar Terrace. Then we'll walk from there."

They made their way through the early morning traffic towards the town's outskirts.

"What's my role in these meetings later, guv?" she asked.

"I want you to observe. Watch and learn. We each have our style. Neil impressed me this week. When you work with him in the future, you'll see him adopt different methods. For me, interviews are like a game of chess. I use an opening gambit. Then I prefer to introduce a shock tactic to put them off balance. It might appear strange, but I want them to think about that instead of their defensive tactics. Anything to get the answers I want."

They had to park a distance from Daphne Tolliver's old house. The scaffolding indicated that the homeowners had decided to make the improvements Wally Tolliver had eschewed for so long.

Gus set off at a leisurely pace to the footpath across the meadow that took them to Battersby Lane. Lydia had to shorten her usual stride to stay beside him. They reached the stile, and Gus clambered over first, then offered his hand to help Lydia negotiate the narrow wooden steps.

"I can manage," she said.

"Did you encounter many stiles in the Scottish cities where you've lived?"

"No, but it's not hard to work out what to do," she replied.

"Touché,"

"Were you talking about me when I fetched the coffee yesterday afternoon?"

"Has that been gnawing away at you for the past eighteen hours?"

"Of course not, but it was obvious when the conversation stopped abruptly as soon as I opened the door."

"Don't take this the wrong way, but what are you wearing under that Barbour?"

"Oh, I get it. This outfit wasn't merely for walking across damp grass and muddy pathways. You expect me to suppress my individuality and conform to the uniform appearance that my male colleagues must display."

"I'd have no objection to Alex or Neil dressing more casually in the office. I don't find what you've worn this week inappropriate, either. However, the public perceives that we should look professional at all times. A uniform helps. A detective in a suit helps. If I turn up in a kaftan, torn jeans and sandals to interview the grieving parent of a stab victim, what message does that send?"

Lydia unzipped her jacket. The orange, red & yellow top almost blinded Gus.

"I got it wrong again, didn't I?" she said. "You need me to dress for the occasion. I get it now."

"Cover yourself up. There may be others enjoying a stroll in the countryside."

"Who in their right mind carries a pair of sunglasses in April on the off chance they need to ward off the sun's glare?"

Gus relaxed. Lydia could take it as well as dish it out. She would prove a valuable asset to the team for as long as they hung on to her.

"This is where Daphne stopped with her dog to talk with someone she knew," said Lydia.

"It was assumed so. Without identifying that person, we can't be sure. After several minutes of chatting, Daphne walked over there to that gap in the hedge. That's where the path runs through to Lowden Park."

"This doesn't match the pictures of the murder site," said Lydia.

"Ten years of growth will have produced a different canopy overhead. Councils have suffered just as severe cuts as the Police. I doubt there's been much of a woodland husbandry programme in place. They will cut down a tree if it dies or becomes a danger to the public. There are hundreds of trees on Lowden Hill. It's not hard to imagine severe damage to several trees thanks to the storms and high winds we've experienced over the years. The undergrowth looks to have been allowed to grow unchecked. The only cutting back is confined to the edges of the pathway. They've preserved the right of way, and that's it."

"Where was the body discovered?"

"I reckon it was over there. Ten paces from the path, behind those oaks."

It was a struggle to reach the trees. The clearing in 2008 was almost covered now in brambles and bracken.

"The still photos of this area suggest that maybe two people could have been here and not be seen by anyone on the path. But, looking back to where Daphne was walking, the massive tree trunks provided an effective screen."

"So, what alerted her? Why did she leave the pathway and come in here?" asked Lydia.

"Someone called out to her. A voice she recognised. Or, perhaps, a noise she overheard and was nosy."

"What were they doing? If it was more than one person?"

"Based on Neil's local knowledge and Pickering's voyeuristic hobby, it doesn't take much imagination. Daphne disturbed a couple having sex. One of those people was young. They may have known Daphne and struck her over the head, killing her. They ran towards the Park, and Holly Wells saw them."

"Who was the other person? Were they young or old? Did *they* know Daphne? Were they male or female?"

"There's something that's been troubling me ever since I picked up the file on this case. This place is renowned for being a lover's haunt. So what? The police will act if we receive a complaint from the public where someone is offending public decency. It's not at the top of the list of things we actively investigate. Thank goodness we still draw the line if children or animals are involved. What made this so important they had to hide its discovery at all costs?"

Gus made his way back to the pathway. There seemed little point following it into Lowden Park, so he and Lydia returned to the car.

Gus prayed Holly Wells might have information to help answer his question.

CHAPTER 9

"We're heading for Barken Road, Chippenham then, guv?"

"Holly lives in a three-bedroomed, older semi-detached house with her husband, Danny and two boys. Both boys will be at school. Danny works in Swindon at the Honda factory."

"Is it okay to open my jacket indoors, guv? It's getting warm."

"I'm sure Holly Wells will be fine with that, Lydia. Just remember. Watch and learn."

Holly stood on the doorstep before they reached the gate.

"Hiya, come on in."

Marriage and motherhood have toughened her up, Gus thought. The file had given the impression of a very nervous young woman.

"Coffee?" asked Holly as soon as they entered the living room door.

"That would be nice," said Gus. "black, no sugar, please."

"Mine's black, with one sugar," said Lydia.

Holly switched on the kettle and fetched mugs from a kitchen wall cabinet.

"So, what did you want to know?" she asked, continuing to chat with them as she took a carton of milk from the fridge.

"My colleague will have told you we're looking into Mrs Tolliver's murder again. My name's Freeman, and this is Lydia Logan Barre. We are part of the Crime Review Team."

Holly brought the two coffees and placed them on china coasters between Gus and Lydia. Then, she returned to the kitchen for her mug.

"It was a terrible time," she said, blowing on her coffee as she walked to a chair opposite them.

"It must have been distressing for you to discover a scene such as that," said Gus. "We wondered whether you remembered any more details about the person you saw running away."

"I stood by the pathway, watching the dog. It kept coming towards me, then scampering back behind the tree into the clearing. I knew something was wrong. Where the other person had been hiding, I don't know. I heard a noise, and as I turned, I caught a glimpse of a blue anorak. The hood was up, and they sprinted off towards the Park."

"You say 'the other person'," said Gus, "did you see two people?"

"Well, no, I only saw one. I screamed when I stepped into the clearing and saw the body."

"A natural reaction," said Gus.

"Yes, but it wasn't just the blood and seeing her eyes staring at the heavens. Instead, I sensed someone watching me. That scared me and made me scream as loud as I did."

That was news to Gus Freeman. Holly hadn't told the detectives this detail back in 2008.

"Let's return to the young person running away from the scene. Can you remember any extra detail of the clothes they wore?"

Lydia leaned forward and looked as if she wanted to speak to Holly. Gus paused.

"Close your eyes, Holly," she said, "try to think of the first thing you noticed."

Holly closed her eyes and breathed out.

"The trainers they wore. They were white and looked brand-new,"

Lydia glanced at Gus. Was this the first time the trainers had been mentioned?

"Go on," said Lydia, "work your way up from there."

"Jeans, stone-washed. Then the blue anorak. Royal blue. There was something odd. I never thought about it at the time. When Danny and I got together, he remarked about my small feet. Size three and a half. We were in a shoe shop in Swindon, and it popped into my head. When I saw that person running, I wasn't sure whether it was a boy or a girl. That's what I told the detective. Danny put his foot next to mine that day in the shop, and his black trainers dwarfed my little feet. Those white trainers were big too, size nine or ten, the same as Danny. That was why I kept having this feeling something didn't feel right. The trainers made me think it was a boy, but the face I saw was more feminine."

"That's very interesting, Holly," said Lydia.

"It certainly is," said Gus, "many thanks for your help and a lovely cup of coffee. We'll let you get on with your day."

Holly walked with them to the door.

"I hope you find the person who did it, Mr Freeman. My Princess never got over the shock. She died within the year."

As they walked to the gate, Holly called out.

"Lydia, I love your top, by the way. I wish I were brave enough to wear something like that."

Gus opened the gate for Lydia. She didn't rebuke him this time.

"Thanks," she said.

"Watch and learn," Gus said with a grin.

Fifteen minutes later, Gus eased his way into the traffic on the M4 at Junction 17.

"Who was Princess?" asked Lydia,

"Holly's Bichon Frise puppy. That's why she visited the Park. We couldn't have expected as much progress as that from her. It puts a whole new complexion on the case."

"I'm sorry that I butted in. I felt Holly's initial answers sounded too much like a repeat of her original statement. By making her stop and consider it differently, I hoped we might get her to remember something she'd forgotten. It worked."

"There were two people in the clearing. One was an effeminate young man. I'm still wondering why this led to murder. We're long past being shocked to hear of two men having sexual relations on Lowden Hill."

"Unless this wasn't a loving relationship," said Lydia, "but prostitution."

"A male prostitute with a client. Yes, that's a distinct possibility. We'll need to continue our investigation into the data provided by the Hub. One shouldn't pre-judge, but I doubt we'll find too many male prostitutes among our thirteen hundred residents. Based on Holly's account, the killer hung around after his partner had fled. He hid in the bushes and slipped away unseen."

"Hang on, guv, that begs the question, doesn't it?"

"Exactly. If it *was* a simple financial transaction, that boy becomes a problem."

"If it became necessary to kill Daphne Tolliver to prevent the liaison from being made public...."

"There were no murders or unexplained deaths in the months that followed. Of course, people leave an area without telling anyone where they're going every day. He could have fled before the killer traced him. We may have misread the situation. They could have been in a long-term relationship, meaning neither man wanted the incident made known. One lashed out and bludgeoned Daphne with a rock. The other ran away. They could be living together in Brighton for all we know. Other seaside resorts are available."

When they arrived at HMP Leyhill, they entered a side room. Percy Pickering was escorted in by an officer. Pickering's face was as grey as his tracksuit top and bottom. Lydia saw his eyes light up as soon as he realised a woman was in the room. She removed her coat and folded it over the back of her chair. She felt unclean when she turned around to see Pickering licking his lips. His tracksuit bottoms showed he was becoming aroused. He didn't take his eyes off her as she sat back on the metal chair opposite him.

"My name is Freeman," said Gus, "a consultant with the Wiltshire Police. My colleague Ms Barre and I wish to discuss what you said you saw on Saturday, the twenty-eighth of June 2008. Your statement in 2013 stated you saw Mrs Tolliver and her dog on Battersby Lane just after seven in the evening. Is that correct?"

"I did see them," replied Pickering.

"Did you photograph them for your collection?"

"No, she was just talking,"

"Who was she talking with?"

"A bloke. Tall, stocky. He crouched to cuddle the dog and knelt on the pavement. The ground was still wet from the earlier rain."

"How old would you say he was?"

"Twenty, maybe, but you had to be daft to kneel in those puddles."

"You didn't recognise him?"

Lydia stretched her back to suggest the metal chairs were uncomfortable.

Pickering swallowed hard.

"I'd seen him around. It was the Attrill lad."

"Attrill?"

"He fell on his head when he was a boy. He wasn't right after that."

"You didn't give us this information when first interviewed, Mr Pickering. Why not?"

"I didn't want to draw attention to myself, did I? I was a mug to come forward after the reconstruction five years ago, but I didn't realise the harm at the time."

"You might have mentioned Attrill's name then. It would have helped us with our enquiries."

Pickering didn't respond. He no longer stared at Lydia. His head was on his chest.

Gus nodded to the prison officer. Pickering was led away to his cell.

"What a pathetic little worm," said Lydia.

"Was that a deliberate attempt to provoke him?" asked Gus.

"These chairs are bloody uncomfortable," she replied.

"That's okay then; I hope you didn't use your feminine wiles to advance our progress. If a defence solicitor had been in the room, he would have pounced on that and claimed harassment."

Lydia scoured his face for the hint of a smile. She saw none. Had she misheard what the three were saying in the office yesterday? She thought Gus had approved of a distraction technique. Men, she'd never understood them.

"We need to trace this Attrill character," said Gus as they drove back to the office.

"Could he be the killer, guv?"

"Attrill spoke with the victim less than half an hour before her murder. Even if he wasn't involved, he might have seen one or both men before they got to the clearing in the woods. Where did the killer slip away to after the killing? Did he reappear on Battersby Lane? Did he move further up Lowden Hill? Where was Attrill then?"

"We're getting closer, guv, aren't we?"

"Who knows? We've uncovered a few nuggets that Culverhouse and his team didn't find. Whether we can make something with them? Only time will tell. When we get back to the office, remember to update the Freeman File with your record of the interviews and our visit to the crime scene. Do it while your memory is still fresh and your notes are still legible. So much has gone on today; this was your first time in the field. It would be easy to forget something in the excitement."

"Thanks, guv. It has been a great experience so far."

"Better than interpreting reams of data from the Hub, I bet."

Alex and Neil were deep into whatever details they were sifting through on their computer screens when they did get upstairs to the office.

"Listen up," said Gus, "we've made two, no, maybe three breakthroughs."

"You two will work together again then," said Neil, his shoulders slumped in mock resignation.

"Lydia got Holly Wells to remember the running man wore white trainers that were size nine or ten. That jibed with her glimpse of the face she had seen partially obscured by the anorak's hood. At first, she believed it could have been a man *or* a woman. But, with hindsight, the shoes convinced her it was a man who might pass as a woman."

"A ladyboy?" asked Neil, "are you serious?"

"A male prostitute or a rent boy, why not?" asked Lydia, "the description Holly gave us fits that profile far better than anything we've come up with before."

"Holly also says her scream wasn't only at the sight of Daphne's body but because she sensed someone lurking in the bushes. She wanted to attract the attention of those close to her in case they posed a threat. That was a new admission. Holly didn't say that before. So we have a killer and his partner, two people, in the clearing. We need to establish a true relationship between these two. Were they two male lovers? Or was it a man who paid for casual sex with the boy, and Daphne recognised him? Either way, she was killed to stop her talking. If the sex was consensual and part of an ongoing relationship, we need to find the young man with the white trainers and royal blue anorak. He's guilty of murder by association. He was present when a murder was committed. If he was a male prostitute who fled the scene, then if Daphne had to die, this young man was in grave danger. Who was he? Where did he go immediately after the attack? Where is he now? Are we looking for a second body?"

"Blimey, you two uncovered a can of worms," said Alex, "it makes our efforts look pedestrian by comparison."

"What did Percy the Pervert come up with," asked Neil.

"Based on the small tent in his tracksuit bottoms, very little," said Lydia.

"When he dragged his eyes away from Ms Barre, he identified the young man in Battersby Lane. He'd known all along, but because his perversions needed keeping under wraps, he only revealed the absolute minimum to Culverhouse. We're looking for a bloke called Attrill, around thirty years old today. As a young boy, he fell on his head and is less advanced in his mental development than his age suggests."

"Call Megan Morris, Neil, and find out if she knows this Attrill. He's local, and if he knew Daphne and Bobby, she'd probably know of him."

"This puts a different slant on the case, doesn't it?" said Alex.

"It does," said Gus, "unless your work today has thrown up new names, then we can virtually eliminate the people on that list of long shots. So, we scrub the ex-colleagues at the Post Office and the volunteers at the Charity shops. Ditto the lady of the Manor and her old retainer, plus the staff at the Primary School. Wally's mates and Daphne's neighbours can rest easy too."

"Megan Morris says his name is Simon," said Neil, replacing the phone. "The kids at the Primary School where Daphne worked used to call him 'Simple Simon'. His mental age is eight. As you suggested, he is thirty and still lives at home with his parents. Megan told me that Daphne had reported the children involved in the name-calling. Their teacher lectured the culprits, and their parents received a letter from the school. That put a stop to that nonsense for a while. Carl Brightwell and the crowd he hung out with bullied Simon Attrill. Most of that has stopped since Carl went to prison. Megan described Simon Attrill as a 'gentle giant'.

"We need to talk to Simon and his parents. To discover if he can tell us anything about the hour after he left Daphne Tolliver on Battersby Lane."

"I believe we'll cross another name off if he fills in the gaps, don't you, guv?" said Neil.

Gus nodded.

Thursday, 12th April 2018

Gus and Lydia left the office at a quarter past nine, leaving Alex and Neil to search social media and discuss the local prostitution scene with colleagues at the new police station.

"What will happen to Simon when his parents are no longer around to care for him, guv?" asked Lydia.

"Over eighty per cent of people in Simon's situation live with their parents until they pass," said Gus. "Community care services help those who need care and support to live with dignity and independence and avoid isolation. The services are aimed at those with a mental illness, learning disability and physical disability. Of course, they won't want to hear it, but the best thing his parents could do would be to prepare Simon for his future without them. There are places in the community where he could live independently, with support on hand when he needed it."

"They wouldn't hear of it, though, I bet."

"Just look at that," said Gus.

Everything about the property they were visiting clashed with its neighbours. The other houses on this Avenue on the Greenwood estate looked drab and unloved. On the other hand, the Attrills front garden was full of flowers. It boasted a water feature and hanging baskets on either side of the door.

Most front gardens on either side of the road had been paved or laid with gravel straying onto the pavements. As a result, many had rusting white goods instead of floral displays. It had become the modern way.

A cheery, red-faced man answered the door. He looked to be the same age as Gus.

"Hello there," he said, "you must be from the police. Come on in."

"Good morning, Mr Attrill. I'm Freeman, a civilian consultant with Wiltshire police. This lady is Ms Barre, one of my colleagues on the Crime Review Team. Is Simon at home?"

"He is; when your people called yesterday afternoon, they said you wished to talk with the three of us. My wife is through here, in the conservatory. Simon is playing in the garden. We can call him in when you're ready."

Mr Attrill led them through the kitchen and into a utility room. A patio door opened into the conservatory that ran the width of the rear of the house. Gus remembered Tess had spoken about adding an extension to their bungalow.

He hadn't been as keen. The way this room faced meant the Attrills had the sun until late evening. It was evident they loved it. There was no escaping the warmth of the sun. If he sat out here for any length of time, he would fall asleep.

Gus and Tess wouldn't have been as fortunate. Their back garden was in the shade by two in the afternoon this time of year. He preferred the open air he enjoyed at his allotment.

Mrs Attrill was a cheery-faced individual too. She jumped up from her chair, letting her knitting drop onto the floor.

"Welcome," she cried, "can I get you something to drink? How about a cool glass of lemonade? Call Simon indoors, darling, will you?"

Mr Attrill went to the conservatory door while his wife scuttled towards the kitchen.

"She likes to keep busy," he said to Gus as he passed, "she won't check if you prefer a hot drink. It's just her way."

"A cold drink will be just fine," said Gus.

He gazed out of the conservatory window. The front garden looked good, but this was great. Every square inch utilised.

Mr Attrill was walking back with Simon now. He had been in the greenhouse in the far right-hand corner. Simon towered over his father and was a giant, as Megan Morris had described him. He shuffled along, holding his father's hand.

"I was watering the plants," said Simon, "who are you?"

"This man and lady are from the police, Simon," his father said as they reached a wooden bench by the door. Simon sat on it. He didn't seem to want to come inside.

"We wanted to ask you about Mrs Tolliver, Simon," said Gus, "do you remember her?"

"I never see her now. I miss playing with Bobby,"

"Do you remember the last time you saw her with Bobby, Simon, on Battersby Lane? It was a long time ago now."

Gus could see Lydia and Mrs Attrill through the window. Simon's mother looked agitated. She wanted to come out to be with her son.

"Let's go inside, Simon. Mum's got a nice glass of lemonade for you. It's a reward for helping me with the watering."

"Thirsty work," said Simon, "The plants get thirsty, too, in the summer."

The three men made their way indoors. Simon sat next to his mother. His father stood to the side and invited Lydia and Gus to sit in the remaining chairs. A pitcher of lemonade and five glasses stood on the glass-topped table in the centre of the room.

Lydia got her first good look at Simon Attrill. He was huge; his hands were the size of dinner plates. His manner was childlike, but his features were those of a thirty-year-old who reminded her of the archetypal farm labourer who spent his days in the open air. He could have been handsome, and yet as soon as he turned his face towards you, the damage done by that dreadful childhood accident was all too plain to see.

"Tastes good," said Simon, smacking his lips after demolishing half a glass in one mouthful.

"Tell Mr Freeman about the last time you saw Bobby, Simon," said his father.

"I got my knees wet. So Mum made me change my trousers when I got home."

"Where was Bobby the last time you played with him, Simon?" asked Gus.

"Going into Lowden Woods. I watched them until I couldn't see them anymore."

"Did anyone else leave the pathway after they had gone?"

"I walked home. I'm not supposed to be out too late,"

"So, nobody was in the Lane or Lowden Hill when you walked home?"

"Only the man, but he was too far away for me to tell who he was," said Simon.

"On the hillside?"

"Now you see him, and now you don't,"

"He disappeared behind the trees. Is that what you mean?"

"Now you see him, and now you don't. Can I go back to finish watering the plants?"

"I think so," said Gus, nodding to Mr Attrill. He took Simon back into the garden.

"You have a beautiful garden, Mrs Attrill. It must take hours to keep it this good," said Lydia.

"My husband describes his garden as a labour of love. He transformed the space from a rough meadow into what we have now. It's been a peaceful haven for over twenty years, and I spent my recovery from a serious illness here. It helps the three of us physically and spiritually. We feel very blessed."

"This garden stops you in your tracks," said Gus. "It must be a joy to live with throughout the year," said Gus, "it puts my garden to shame."

"I don't even know what all the flowers are," admitted Lydia, "I'm a city girl."

"We've got red-hot pokers, allium, ornamental lilies, begonias and freesias. I like the gravel paths that zig-zag through the beds. We plant the vegetables among the flowering plants. Simon loves the colours and finding cabbages and lettuces hidden behind a hydrangea. It's an adventure every day for him."

Mr Attrill had returned. He stood in the patio doorway.

"Is that it, then?" he asked.

"He confirmed what we knew: that he was the last person to see Daphne Tolliver alive, apart from her killer. The man he saw in the trees up on Lowden Hill was most likely responsible and is one of two men we now wish to identify as soon as possible. Simon was at least a hundred yards away from the person on the hill. He says he couldn't tell who it was. Unless he knew him very well, it's unlikely he could tell at that distance. I think it's everything we can hope to learn from him. We're very grateful for your cooperation, both of you."

Mr and Mrs Attrill walked to the front door with Gus and Lydia. They stood on the doorstep and watched until they drove away.

"It's so sad, isn't it?" said Lydia, "it's as if he's still eight in their eyes. They don't treat him as an adult. Surely, it would be better for his future if they prepared him for what's coming?"

"Simon's mother said the garden helped her recover when she was seriously ill. Perhaps it was a mental illness, and she's never come to terms with what happened. Simon's father may be the only one with a grip on reality in that household."

"Where would the man have been heading from that point on the hillside?"

"Search me. Anywhere on the Westbourne estate, the town centre itself and surrounding villages. He could have had a car nearby."

"We're no further forward, then?"

"I asked if there was anybody on the hillside. Simon said it was a man. We now know for certain it wasn't a woman. Would he have said boy if it had been someone Gavin or Carl's age? I believe so. He would have associated them with someone only a few years older than himself. But, in his eyes, he saw someone who was a man, even then. Over twenty-one."

"Our next port of call will be a different experience," said Lydia.

"The Manor House? The sooner we get this over, the better. Alex reckons the General Manager has dementia. He was the chef when Daphne Tolliver began working there. The Minister's wife has a reputation for liking a drink. We'd better get over there before she starts swigging the sherry."

The Manor House was an imposing property. Gus had needed to interview the odd Lord and Lady in his time. Usually, after a burglary or there had been poachers on their estate. He parked the Ford Focus on the far side of the stone steps leading to the front door.

"A longer walk this way, guv," said Lydia.

"I thought it best not to lower the tone by parking my jalopy slap-bang in the middle of the driveway. I know my place."

"Do you approve of my outfit today, guv?"

"I had noticed. The Attrill's garden had more show of colour than you, which makes a change. You only need to tone it down, Lydia. Maybe the classy Mrs Pemberton-Smythe will give you a few pointers."

Lydia was on the verge of taking issue with her boss. But, as she turned towards him, she saw he had a twinkle in his eye.

"Touché," she quipped.

Gus rang the bell. His hand was poised to ring again when it opened. A short, fat woman in a black dress and wearing a white apron looked at them.

"Please?" she said. Gus wasn't sure whether she was Spanish or Italian.

"We are here to speak with Isaac Crompton. It's the police. We have an appointment."

"Please?" the lady repeated and waved them into the large hallway.

"I think we're supposed to wait," said Lydia.

The lady of unknown Mediterranean origin strolled away to the rooms on the right-hand side of the staircase.

Gus heard her knock on a wooden door. She went inside, and thirty seconds later, she reappeared.

"Please?" she said more loudly, so they heard her and beckoned them to come forward.

"Crompton must be along here, I assume," said Gus, "I wonder what we'll find."

They almost reached the doorway when they heard a cultured voice call out.

"If you wish to interrogate Crompton, he should have a responsible adult present. I'm the only one who can get any sense out of him these days."

This must be Joyce Pemberton-Smythe, Gus thought.

"Good morning," said Gus, "I'm Freeman. I'm attached to Wiltshire Police as a consultant looking into the Daphne Tolliver murder in 2008. My colleague is Ms Barre."

"Poor old Daffers. We do miss her. Thank you, Maria. You can hurry back to the kitchen now. I'm sure there's plenty for you to do."

With a brief bob of her head, the servant accepted she should leave.

"Maria joined us eighteen months ago. She came highly recommended by the agency. Unfortunately, my Portuguese is non-existent, and her English hasn't progressed much."

"Please," said Lydia.

"Exactly. Maria makes it cover pretty much everything. Most Brits are just as bad when they travel overseas, so we can't complain. I speak French like a native, but Maria didn't get much schooling in Rio de Janeiro."

"Who's that?" A disembodied voice came from beyond the open door.

"Only me, Crompton," said Joyce, and she entered the room. Gus and Lydia followed her.

Crompton sat in a window seat overlooking the lawns to the side of the Manor House. He had a beautiful view of the Italian garden beyond, and Gus could see the vast expanse of Lowden Hills in the distance. Despite the warmer weather, Crompton had a rug covering him below the waist.

"Crompton, these are the people I mentioned yesterday. They want to talk to you about Daphne. Mrs Tolliver. Do you remember?"

Crompton had been studying each of them, one by one. Finally, he turned towards the window.

"Daphne," he said, "she asked me to call her Daphne, not Mrs Tolliver. That was a long time ago. I miss talking to her."

"How long has he been like this?" Gus asked quietly.

"Around eighteen months ago, I noticed his short-term memory was on the blink. That's why we employed Maria. We couldn't rely on him to cook our meals on time. When my husband is home, we are on a tight schedule. Of course, we entertain guests, and Crompton's vague grip on things left us with empty plates and bemused guests on several occasions. Your Chief Constable was among them. He plays golf at North Wilts with Leonard."

"Do you mind if we check a few things ourselves," asked Gus, "he remembers Mrs Tolliver from ten years ago. All may not be lost. Was there any reason he didn't leave here and seek treatment elsewhere?"

"Look, I am aware of what ordinary people think of us who still have staff waiting on us hand and foot," said Joyce Pemberton-Smythe. It was the most animated she had been since they arrived. She walked over to Crompton and placed her hand on the older man's shoulder. "He's been part of Leonard's family for fifty years. He came straight from the Savoy at twenty-one to work for Leonard's father. Crompton became indispensable as our General Manager. When his eyesight began to fail, we employed a series of cleaners. Daffers was the first. Nobody since has been as conscientious. As far as Leonard and I are concerned, old Crompton has a home here for as long as he wishes."

"Point taken," said Gus, "we'll be as careful as we can with him."

Joyce sat beside Crompton on the window seat.

"Do you know what day it is, Crompton?"

"Every day's the same," said the old man.

"Do you know what year it is?

"I'm over seventy now, you know. It has to be Twenty Sixteen, hasn't it? Does it matter?"

"Not really," said Gus, "what about our Prime Minister?"

"What about her? She's not a patch on Maggie Thatcher."

Lydia looked around the room. The furniture was superior to what she expected a servant to enjoy. Crompton's status in the household matched Joyce's passionate outburst.

There were only two photos on display. One was a family photo, with the four Pemberton-Smythes in a professionally shot pose. It didn't say Christmas 2017 at the bottom, but the two sons looked early to mid-twenties. So it had to be recent.

The other was older, whereas Leonard looked ten or fifteen years younger. He sat in an office with wood-panelled walls. Might that be his Westminster office? She walked across and picked it up.

"Could you tell us who is in this photograph, Crompton," she asked.

"Mr Leonard," replied Crompton, "surely you recognise your local MP? He's a Junior Minster."

"Leonard's Secretary of State for Justice now, Crompton," said Joyce, "don't you remember me telling you?"

"Oh, yes, I remember now."

"Can you tell us what this item is?" asked Lydia, pointing to an umbrella in a wooden hat and coat stand in the corner of the office.

"Umbrella. Blue. Leonard's a Tory. He wouldn't be seen dead with a red one."

"How about this?"

The item in the photo was a white mobile phone.

"One of those fancy new phones. We use a proper one here."

"Crompton means the landline in the hall. It's not the old black Bakelite type these days. Although it is one of the slimline models from the Seventies, Leonard and I use smartphones, but Crompton wouldn't know that. No reason why he should."

Gus had looked at the photo to gauge what Lydia aimed at when she first chose it. It made sense to check whether Crompton still had a grasp on recognising everyday items. He found his eyes wandering back to the photo. What made him look twice? It would come to him in time.

"Let's discuss Daphne, Isaac," said Gus.

Crompton sat bolt upright.

"He never uses that name," said Joyce, "it reminds him of his parents. They strongly believed in spare the rod and spoil the child. Crompton had a terrible time of it."

"Daphne," said Crompton, "I miss her company."

"When did you last see her?" asked Gus.

"She doesn't work here now. So Millie does the cleaning now. She's lazy."

"Lasted a month," said Joyce, "I've lost count. Let me think. There have been five since Daffers. I don't think you'll be fortunate, Mr Freeman."

Gus agreed.

"Perhaps we can go somewhere else, madam? So we can talk to you in private?"

"Of course," said Joyce, moving away from Crompton. "I'll get Maria to serve us coffee in the conservatory."

Crompton realised his mistress was leaving and tried to stand. The rug slipped to the floor.

"Oh, Crompton, not again," said Joyce. The older man wasn't wearing any trousers. Lydia was thankful he'd put on his underpants.

Joyce ran back to help him sit back on the seat. She tucked the rug around his stick-thin legs.

"It must be Thursday," said Crompton, "I always bathe on a Thursday night."

CHAPTER 10

As they left Isaac Crompton in his room, Gus hoped he went the same way as Tess without warning. He couldn't face a long, lingering death where he didn't have his faculties.

Lydia was at Freeman's shoulder. She thought how lucky Crompton was in his hour of need to have Joyce Pemberton-Smythe caring for him. Leonard, her husband, had a reputation for being keen on family values. Joyce upheld those values here at the Manor House.

After they relocated to the conservatory, Joyce summoned Maria. The coffee duly arrived, and once again, the chubby Brazilian cook made a half-hearted attempt at a curtsey as she made her exit.

"Right," said Joyce, "what can I tell you?"

"Do you recall where Crompton was the day of the murder?" asked Gus.

"Crompton was here. He's always been here. It's difficult to remember what happened that weekend. My memory isn't what it was. The demon drink had a role to play there. The Priory helped me in that regard."

The Priory was news to Gus. Alex Hardy hadn't added that titbit to the Freeman File. But, of course, people with addiction were unlikely to broadcast the fact they underwent treatment. It went some way to explaining how she appeared so lucid today. He'd expected her to be hungover and suffering from the shakes.

"I started keeping a diary a year before Daffers came to work for us," Joyce continued.

"Do you have the diary for June 2008?" asked Gus, perking up. So this meeting might not be a lost cause, after all.

"I have, but those diaries contain things I wouldn't wish to find their way into the gutter press. Leonard is on the verge of being promoted to Home Secretary. Any whiff of my struggles with alcohol back then would scupper any hopes he has of getting the top job in the future. You do understand?"

"Might I remind you we're reviewing a murder case, madam? The police can be discreet on these matters."

"I appreciate that, but unless you have a court order, I must insist that I only reveal the events I noted for the weekend of Daphne's death."

Gus decided he could work with the weekend details for now. If it led to something pertinent to the case, he would be back with Geoff Mercer and a warrant to search the premises.

"Leonard returned home late on Friday night. The House had sat until seven. A Tory Member had taken his seat that day. He'd just won a by-election, and Leonard had a drinks party with him and a few others. We breakfasted together in the morning and discussed our plans. Most MPs hold surgeries in their constituency weekly to allow people to meet them and discuss matters of concern. Leonard has an office in the town where he attends for as long as people wait. Because that is rather open-ended, I would pop into Bath to go shopping. On occasion, we dined out in the evening, but by and large, Crompton saw to our evening meals."

"Did you travel to Bath that day?" asked Gus.

"I didn't make a note of it, no."

"What time did your husband return from his surgery?"

"I drew a blank on that one, I'm afraid. All I had scribbled in the margin was a question mark. We breakfasted together in the morning quite early for a Sunday. Leonard dashed off to North Wilts for an early tee-off time with his chums. I imagine we dined together later in the afternoon, and then he travelled to London. An unremarkable yet typical weekend *chez nous.*"

"Your husband lives in London during the week, is that correct?" asked Gus.

"He does," said Joyce, "his prolonged absences accelerated my unhealthy level of drinking back in the day. The boys were at boarding school. Leonard was in his apartment, wheeling and dealing his way to high office. Little old Joyce only had Crompton to keep her company during the day. He kept himself to himself in the evenings."

"Were you ever tempted?" asked Gus.

Joyce looked shocked.

"With Crompton. Heavens no. How gross."

"Forgive me, I was thinking of a younger man. Crompton's duties as General Manager saw him invite workers and tradespeople to the Manor House. An attractive woman. Lonely. It's not unheard of for the occasional liaison to occur, so I hear."

Joyce laughed.

"I take my marriage vows seriously, Mr Freeman. My husband and I have an unconventional marriage by some standards, but it works for us. I rarely met the people Crompton hired to work outside. If there was any decorating to the interior, he scheduled it for the summer months when we holidayed in France. I chatted with Daphne from time to time. She would finish her cleaning duties and make an excuse to pop in here before she left. She ran a duster over the window sills and plumped up the cushions. Often she would wake me up and check I was okay before she trotted off home. She never passed judgement on the odd vodka bottle she found under the cushions. Daffers was a gem."

Gus couldn't think of another question to ask.

"There are very few people as loyal and trustworthy as Daphne," Joyce continued, "thinking back to your question about the workmen. Crompton had an odd habit. He felt duty-bound to offer contracts for mowing the lawns, for instance, to different firms each year. The same with gardeners, window cleaners, and so on. The only person he religiously stuck to for supplying us with our hanging baskets was a Mr Attrill."

"We've met him. He has a beautiful garden," said Lydia.

"Mr Attrill and his son, Simon, have been coming here for years," said Joyce, "Daphne knew Simon. I would see her talking with him outside the window after she'd left me. She was so good with him. I must admit he rather frightens me. Such a big man."

"When would Simon and his father visit the Manor House?" asked Gus.

"We have baskets throughout the year. They call in from time to time. I don't think they had any fixed agreement on the number of visits per year. Crompton won't remember now, I'm afraid. I could ask Mr Attrill if it's important."

"No, that's fine," said Gus, "that's it for now. If we need more, we'll call and make another appointment. Perhaps when your husband is at home."

"You can always drop into his surgery office on a Saturday. He's bound to be there. As for Sunday, do you play golf?"

"I do not, and if the Chief Constable is in a regular foursome with your husband, I wouldn't be popular if I turned up with my notebook asking questions."

Joyce walked to the hallway with Gus and Lydia. On a table near the foot of the stairs lay a pile of magazines and newspapers. Joyce flicked through them.

"There's an article in here on Leonard. It's a local monthly magazine; they photographed him in his surgery office. I prefer this more distinguished look to Crompton's older one in his quarters. You can keep the rag. I've read it. Goodbye now. I hope to hear via the Chief Constable that you've caught Daphne's killer soon."

Gus and Lydia said their goodbyes. As they descended the steps to the car, Gus thought what a transformation Joyce had turned out to be from the woman he had expected to meet.

"Back to the office, guv?" said Lydia.

"Let's flick through this magazine first. Here we are — our local MP in his constituency office. No umbrella. Many lever-arch files filled with paperwork, a blue mobile phone, and a box of tissues. Jacket off, shirt-sleeves rolled up to suggest he's hard at work on behalf of us all, regardless of who we voted for."

"A strange morning," said Lydia as they pulled away and drove out of the gates of the Manor House.

"Very interesting, though," said Gus, "very interesting indeed."

Friday, 13th April 2018

Gus motored into work after a good night's sleep. Yesterday afternoon had been a time to regroup to assess what they had learned from the various interviews they had carried out.

He knew that today Geoff Mercer would be in touch for a progress report on the case. What should he tell him? Whatever he passed on to Geoff reached the ears of the ACC. If Kenneth Truelove were true to his word, this Crime Review Team wouldn't be micro-managed. Gus could run it his way. However, it never paid to be too hasty.

Sometimes, it was better to drip-feed information to your superiors. When you were young and inexperienced, it was easy to brag about how well you had done. Look what we've discovered. We're almost ready to make an arrest.

Those cases blew up in your face, leaving egg on it.

Something you thought you had nailed down drifted away in the wind.

Gus was too experienced to fall into that trap. That was why he got Lydia and the two lads to get the Freeman File together after lunch.

Then they stopped and confirmed the new items they could prove since the team had started work on Monday.

He had asked them to shout out the 'definite' items so he could write them on the board.

"Nobody in the Morris family was involved in Daphne's murder."

"Simon Attrill was the person in Battersby Lane seen talking to Daphne."

"There was a man on the hillside, leaving the murder scene in the opposite direction to Lowden Park."

"The other person at the murder scene who ran towards the Park had big feet."

He had looked at Neil.

"Really? Foot size was the only verifiable fact in that part of the enquiry?"

"Sorry, guv, but that's all we can legitimately say," said Neil. "We assume it's a bloke who could pass for a girl. But, of course, it could still be a girl with big feet."

Gus had to agree.

Lydia spoke next.

"We now understand the connections between things from the interviews we had with the Attrills, Crompton and Mrs Pemberton-Smythe. Whether any of those connections bring us closer to identifying the killer, we don't know."

"How significant is it that Simon works at the Manor House?" he had asked.

"It adds another dimension to the relationship between him and Daphne," said Lydia.

"Daphne stood up for him at the Primary School," added Alex. "They spoke whenever they met on her walks with Bobby. Simon talked to her at the Manor House when he and his father tended to the hanging baskets they supplied."

Somewhat chastened by the conclusions they could draw in the cold light of day, he had asked Alex and Neil to take him through what they discovered while he was away.

That had been his last resort. They might progress if they could pin down the person's identity in the woods that Holly saw.

Just before going-home time, Alex had told him the Hub turned up three names. Two fell within the age range Lydia requested from the most recent census. They were residents of the area and aged between eighteen and twenty-four years at the time of the murder. The third was someone who had moved into the area months before the killing.

All three appeared on the later search request as having been known to the police. Consequently, the offences they had in common were relevant to the case.

Despite the date, Gus hoped today would lead to them making that final step.

As he parked his Ford Focus next to Lydia's Mini, he wondered, could they discover which of those three men was the running man?

His team were upstairs and hard at work when he arrived.

Three heads rose when he reached his desk and paused in their labours as he sat on the edge and threw his arms open wide.

"Give me the good news," he said, "please."

"We checked social media for physical descriptions of the three men the Hub indicated were possible suspects," Neil replied. "In 2008, they all displayed the typical characteristics of a twink."

"That in itself doesn't move us forward much," added Alex.

"You're telling me they have big feet and could pass as a female. Terrific."

"To be more specific," said Lydia, "images that are still online show them to be physically attractive with little or no body or facial hair. They were slim to average build, and one had a youthful appearance that belied his older chronological age."

"Taking them one by one, in no particular order, guv. Ricky Edmunds was nineteen years old," Neil continued, "he lived in Harrington End. He had been working as a male prostitute for a year."

Neil pinned a picture of a young Ricky onto one of the notice boards. He was bare-chested, jeans slung low on narrow hips. His feet were out of shot.

"Where is Ricky now," asked Gus.

"Swindon, guv. He lives in a flat and continues to be a sex worker."

"Ricky and up to twenty thousand other men are making an honest living the same way," said Lydia, "he advertises through apps and websites. He offers a range of services, from massages to sexual intercourse. Clients can visit him at his flat, or he can stay overnight at their home or hotel room. What Ricky's doing is legal."

"Exactly," said Gus, "it only becomes illegal when someone sells themselves against their will, solicits for work or keeps a brothel."

"Ricky states in his online adverts that unsafe sex and the use of drugs are unacceptable."

"A visit to Swindon for you two lads, then," said Gus, "visit Ricky Edmunds and question him over his whereabouts on the day of the murder. Just because he now purports to operate a squeaky-clean business doesn't mean he didn't like it rough as a youngster."

"Our second local figure is Joe Walker, twenty-one at the time," said Neil. "He lived in a flat above a hairdresser's in Market Square. Walker received a caution for loitering late at night near public toilets and talking with revellers as they left the late-night bars."

"We only have photos of Joe as he looked in the past five years," said Alex. "He was on Facebook earlier, but his history from before 2013 is sketchy. Either he didn't often post back then, or he's deleted posts because they don't show him in a great light."

"Where is Joe living now?" asked Gus.

"Warminster, guv, he's married to an ex-squaddie, Gerald, thirty-seven. They've adopted twin boys aged eighteen months. There are more photos of the loving family than of Joe as a young man. Joe is a househusband, and Gerald has a well-paid job in recruiting. Joe's previous sex work is history."

"Lydia and I will take that one," said Gus.

"You might want to rethink that, guv," said Alex, "here's the most recent photo of Joe, Gerald and the boys."

Joe Walker's skin was smooth and clean-shaven. His mother may have been born and bred in the county, but his father's heritage belonged in the Caribbean.

"Two steps forward and three steps back," moaned Gus, "this Hub facility isn't much use, is it?"

"Be fair, guv," said Lydia, "Joe Walker was in the right age bracket, known to the police and prone to prostituting himself. We didn't ask the Hub to filter for ethnicity."

"Wheel out number three, then. Unless the guy is an eight-foot-tall Russian weight-lifter," said Gus.

"Mark Richards was twenty-five at the time of the murder. He moved into the area around March 2008. Born in Kidderminster, he moved to Birmingham at age seventeen. His first caution came on Soho Road. Mark had moved to London by 2006. Initially, there were instances where Richards fell foul of the law, but throughout 2007 he was invisible. Mark's social media posts on several sites were of little use in explaining where he worked, socialised or holidayed. Instead, his online activity consisted of sharing or retweeting other people's original material."

"It sounds like he had something to hide," Gus said.

"Or, he was just boring," said Lydia.

"Where did he live when he travelled west? Where did he work? When can we talk to him?"

"He worked as a cocktail waiter at The Beeches motel on the outskirts of town," said Neil, "and he lived on the premises. The Beeches was a dump, to be fair. The locals would frequent the bar up there at one time because they had entertainment, particularly at the weekends. That died out in the Nineties. When Richards worked there, only travelling salesmen and unmarried couples used the place."

"Given his background, what was the attraction for Richards?" asked Gus.

"Following up on what you mentioned, guv, he could have been in hiding," said Alex.

"Was he a user?" asked Lydia.

"Nothing noted in the Hub's report," said Alex.

"Perhaps he's a recovering addict," suggested Gus, "or he picked up something nasty in the city. Anyway, Lydia and I can ask him when we contact him."

Neil puffed out his cheeks.

Gus was getting used to Neil's mannerisms. He wasn't about to hear good news.

"Don't tell me, Neil," said Gus.

"The Beeches closed at the end of June 2008. Several of the staff that lived in stayed on for a while. Finally, the owners tried to sell the place as a going concern. We don't know what happened to Richards after that. However, he didn't appear in our region in the 2011 Census."

"So, we don't have an image of Richards from around ten years ago to show to Holly Wells?"

"No, guv,"

Gus counted the options off on his fingers.

"Did he ever apply for a passport? Did he have a driving licence? Do his parents still live in Kidderminster? Come on, think outside the box. There must be a photo of this bloke somewhere in this bloody country."

Gus felt the vibration of his mobile in his jacket pocket. Here comes trouble.

"Hello?"

It was Superintendent Geoff Mercer, his drinking buddy.

"Yes, Sir. I'll be there in thirty minutes."

Gus ended the call.

"I'm heading for a meeting in the London Road offices. I'll be back as soon as I can. Keep digging. Try Kidderminster first. Also, find out where Richards lived and worked when he lived in London. Did he always work in jobs associated with cafes, bars, and nightclubs? You know what questions to ask. There are plenty of opportunities for a young person to get up to mischief in a big city. What happened in 2007 that stopped him from drawing the attention of the police?"

Gus headed for the lift, then he stopped and turned.

"My gut instinct is that of the three names the Hub came up with, Richards is the only likely candidate for our running man. There are questions I want to ask this guy when we find him. He left a sizable Worcestershire town for the bright lights of Birmingham at seventeen. Then he switched to the capital, where so many had gone before him expecting to find the streets paved with gold. After eighteen months largely spent under the radar, he moved to a quiet West Country town to work at a failing motel at twenty-five years of age. That does not compute, boys and girl."

Gus left them to ponder on that and headed for the car park. Geoff Mercer wanted an update. He had thirty minutes to get his shit together.

Back in the office, the team followed up on Gus's enquiries and reflected on how this case had changed.

"I'll chase up Ricky Edmunds and fix up a date and time for us to meet him," said Neil.

"I'll search for this Richards guy's family in Kidderminster," said Alex.

"Looks as if I'll be hunting the photographic evidence that Mark Richards exists," said Lydia.

"What a change in Joe Walker's life," said Alex. "When he was cottaging back in his teens, you could have got long odds he'd be in a loving relationship with children inside a decade."

"Decades ago, we did our utmost to stop gay men having sex in public toilets and outdoor cruising places," said Neil, for Lydia's benefit. "Men frequently got arrested, prosecuted and often jailed."

"The boss said that you don't look for people having sex in public places these days," Lydia replied.

"We don't," said Alex, "the police only get involved when bystanders complain. That doesn't only apply to gay people. Straight people have also enjoyed sex in secluded spots, haven't they, Neil?"

"You won't let me forget that will you?"

"There's a new term for this now," said Alex, "PSE - Public Sex Environments. For instance, you can still commit an offence in a PSE, like outraging public decency or exposure. It isn't straightforward. Sex in Lowden Woods is different from a couple having sex on a crowded beach at Bournemouth. Both can still be interpreted as public places."

"So, what do we think happened when Daphne Tolliver was in Lowden Woods?" asked Lydia.

"If Mark Richards is our man, then she caught him having sex with another man."

"This goes back to what the boss said earlier. It looks more likely that it was consensual sex and, therefore, completely legal. So, why was she killed?"

"There's no evidence to suggest Daphne ever met Mark Richards," said Alex. "The man Simon Attrill saw hurrying away in the opposite direction to Richards has to be a local that Daphne recognised."

"There aren't many of those we haven't eliminated," said Neil.

Meanwhile, Gus pulled into the visitor's car park at the Police HQ in Devizes. The yellow Spider was three spaces to his left. Vera was in the building. He signed in at Reception. There were no odd looks at the way he dressed today. He slipped the Visitor's Pass over his head and took the stairs two at a time.

Kassie Trotter looked up and gave him a big smile.

"Is Geoff Mercer's office the dark cupboard at the end of the corridor?" he asked.

"Cheeky," she said and nodded.

Gus tapped on the door and waltzed straight into the room.

"In a rush, are we, Freeman?"

It was the big cheese — the Chief Constable.

"Very sorry, Sir. I thought Superintendent Mercer was in here."

"Mercer popped along the corridor to the Gents. I wanted to catch up with you. See how things were progressing."

"We couldn't be happier with the facilities we have available, Sir," Gus said, with his fingers crossed behind his back. "The new offices are super, and the support from the Hub has been exemplary."

"Glad to hear it, Freeman."

Geoff Mercer re-entered the room.

"Hello there, Gus," he said, "let's take a seat, shall we? Can you bring us up to speed with the case?"

"Early days. A case that Dominic Culverhouse and his squad couldn't crack would never be straightforward. We have conducted over a dozen interviews and successfully eliminated several possible explanations. You know my methods. That's why you were so keen to get me back here. My last performance appraisal painted me as dogged. We intend to rest up over the weekend and pursue further enquiries next week. I might have a clearer picture then."

"Was it necessary to interview Joyce Pemberton-Smythe and her staff, Freeman? I'm golfing with our MP on Sunday morning. It's bad enough that Leonard usually takes twenty quid off me. He'll be demanding to learn how you could imagine either of them was involved in this dreadful affair."

"I found Joyce to be a great help and amiable, and Daphne worked with her for some time. So it was a legitimate line of enquiry. But, as I said, we have eliminated several possible explanations."

"I hope so, Freeman. Leonard's reputation as a hard-liner on crime is well known. He's sensitive about a historical murder in his constituency receiving adverse publicity. Rumours that the police are floundering, not knowing where to search for the likely culprit, could damage him."

"I'm sure they would," agreed Gus.

"I know you'll do the right thing, Freeman. Start looking into the criminal elements in the area back then. Your killer will be among them; you mark my words."

The Chief Constable strolled towards the door. He nodded to Geoff Mercer.

When the door closed, Geoff leaned back in his chair.

"That was the biggest load of bullshit I've ever heard, Gus. So, what is the real situation?"

Gus repeated the list of items they had agreed on yesterday afternoon were confirmed new facts. He added Mark Richards to the list, convinced he was the running man. He didn't tell Geoff he believed Mark Richards was dead. Enquiries would continue early next week, but Daphne's killer had to have disposed of the only other witness to her murder.

"Will you be seeing the ACC later?" he asked.

Geoff nodded.

"Do you have anything to tell me yet on the Cambrai Terrace affair?"

"I passed it on to the local officers," Geoff replied, "they're carrying out night surveillance over the weekend. A drone will overfly the site at dusk and dawn tomorrow morning, checking the heat signature. In addition, an undercover team will record anyone entering and leaving the lane. It could take a while, but initial reports suggest something *unusual* shall we say."

"I hope Vera will forgive me if it turns out Monty Jennings is a bit of a rascal," Gus said.

"No need to fret on that score. Vera's known Monty's been a rogue for donkey's years," laughed Geoff.

"Anything else you want from me?"

"Nothing comes to mind. Are you going back to the office?"

Gus nodded.

"How's the team bedding in?"

"You chose well with Alex and Neil. They're solid citizens. Ms Barre is very bright, although I don't want you to spread that around. I want to hold on to her for as long as possible beyond this case. The ACC didn't specify how many other cases he had lined up for the CRT to review. Any ideas?"

"If you crash and burn by upsetting the Chief Constable and his chums, that won't concern you. But, if you remain stubborn and determined and find the killer, then I can think of five unsolved murders in the past twenty years that need a touch of Freeman magic."

Gus shook his head.

"I thought you enjoyed being back doing what you do best?"

"I am, but my allotment is going to suffer."

"Get off with you. We'll meet again this time next week. Then, maybe next weekend, I can wangle a night out for a beer. Is that okay with you?"

"I look forward to it."

"You've got this weekend to yourself, Gus. So why not see what Vera's doing one night? Remember what I said. It doesn't have to be serious. Just a quiet drink. Slow steps."

The two men shook hands, and Gus left the office to walk back along the corridor. He could hear female voices up ahead.

Kassie Trotter's voice was loudest. Vera Jennings could be the other half of the conversation. Unfortunately, her reply was more difficult to catch.

Kassie spotted him as soon as he emerged from the corridor into the small open-plan administration area. Gus hoped the ACC wasn't hovering behind his closed door, waiting to pounce. Geoff could update him in due course. If another top brass figure warned him about not upsetting Leonard Pemberton-Smythe, he'd blow his top.

"Are you rushing away so soon?" asked Kassie.

"Mr Freeman's a busy man," said Vera Jennings.

"Not too busy to talk to us, are you, Mr Freeman?" Kassie said with a smile.

Gus wondered whether he had been wise to trust that this garrulous young woman would appreciate the meaning of a clandestine meeting. He'd warned her that their late-night chat must stay under wraps.

The last person he wanted to be suspicious of his interest in her soon-to-be ex-husband was only a few feet away. That was disturbing enough, yet her green eyes were on full beam and directed towards him.

"As you were in Devizes, we wondered whether you were slipping off home early," said Vera, "TGIF and all that. No doubt you have loads to catch up on now that you've returned to work."

"No rest for the wicked," said Gus. "My team might imagine finishing before five this evening, but I want to achieve the maximum progress on this cold case review. The victim deserves nothing less."

A phone rang. Kassie answered. She stood with a deep sigh and headed for an office on the other side of the floor.

"Our beloved DCI needs another urgent matter dealt with," she called over her shoulder. "No rest, you said. That bit's right. They keep us so busy up here there's little chance of being wicked, though."

Gus watched Kassie rap on the office door and sweep inside.

"She's a character," said Vera.

"She is that," Gus replied, "your assumption I have plenty to catch up on is correct. Much of that can wait until tomorrow. After a busy week, I wouldn't mind the opportunity to relax over a quiet drink later this evening. What do you say?"

"Are you inviting me out, Mr Freeman?"

"I don't see anyone else standing here. Can we dispense with the formalities? It's Gus."

Vera laughed.

"Very well, Gus, but can I suggest we use a place where neither of us is well-known?"

"I'm no Brad Pitt, but surely you're not ashamed to be seen in my company?"

"Look, we both know how people talk. You went out with Geoff Mercer in town last Friday. He must have mentioned my situation. I have three weeks to go before my divorce."

"Vera, it's just a quiet drink. That drink with Geoff was my first social evening since my wife died."

"I'm sure she wouldn't have wanted you to shut yourself off from the world altogether. I was surprised to see you and Geoff enjoying yourselves. The talk flying around when rumours started that you might be coming back suggested you would be at each other's throats."

"We've both mellowed, it appears. I found I quite liked the bloke. Funny old world."

Kassie was on her way back to her desk.

"Still here, Mr Freeman?"

"Just leaving, Kassie,"

"I'll walk to Reception with you," said Vera, "I need to see someone on the Ground Floor."

News to me, thought Kassie. What did I miss? She watched them chatting as they made their way down the stairs and smiled. Mr Freeman had told her he wasn't interested. Crafty devil. Lucky Vera. All I've got to look forward to this weekend is a box set binge of 'Friends' that I bought myself at Christmas.

"Here's my number," said Vera, handing Gus a card at the foot of the stairs, "why don't we say the Waggon & Horses in Harrington End? Nine o'clock?"

"I take it that's not one of your usual haunts?"

"I went there with Monty years ago and more recently with my girlfriends. Do you know it?"

"Not a clue, but my satnav will. Nine o'clock it is then, Vera."

Vera waited until Gus had signed out and reached his car, and then she climbed the stairs back to her desk. Kassie was busy dealing with whatever task the DCI had given her. She kept glancing across, trying to make eye contact. She wanted to know what was going on. But Kassie Trotter would have to wait. Vera was unsure where this quiet drink would lead, but finding out might be fun.

CHAPTER 11

The trip back to the Old Police Station passed in a blur. Gus couldn't have told anyone how much traffic was on the road or the state of the weather. Finally, he reached the door to the lift and reminded himself that he needed to put on his game face by the time he arrived on the first floor.

The image of Vera faded slightly but refused to disappear. As he exited the lift, all those piercing green eyes remained.

"How did the grilling go, guv," asked Neil.

"As well as could be expected," Gus replied, "more important, what have you achieved in my absence?"

"Ricky Edmunds has agreed to meet with us on Monday morning, guv," said Alex.

"He has a lie-in on a Monday," added Neil, "Sunday is always one of his busy periods. So we can talk to him at his gaff at eleven o'clock."

"Poor thing must be tired if he needs to lie in that late," said Gus. "We may hold that interview over depending on what you've learned about Richards."

"Mark Richards has never applied for a passport, and he's never held even a provisional licence, guv," said Lydia.

"His parents are a bigoted pair," said Neil, "he left home because of their reaction to him coming out. Their religion played a big part in that. I couldn't listen to the bile, his old man shouted down the phone. Safe to say, they aren't in a rush to see him come home. So, I tried another angle. I found his sister, Vanessa, through social media. She moved out when she was twenty. Six years after Mark."

"That makes her two, maybe three years younger, right?" asked Gus.

"Vanessa was fourteen when Richards left home, yes."

"Where did the sister move to?"

"The bright lights. Vanessa went to London. Mark was living in Camden Town. They shared a flat from 2006 until he moved west at the end of February 2008. Mark told her he was moving to Wiltshire. She knew his life was complicated. They had argued over how he had earned a living when he first left home and escaped to Birmingham. But, since she'd been in London, he seemed to have got his life together. He worked as a barman in a nightclub. Camden Town is famous for its market, a rabbit warren of fashion and curiosities by the Regent's Canal. There's a thriving nightlife — live music in alternative clubs and old-school pubs. The Jazz Cafe and the Roundhouse are on your doorstep. The capital is in the grip of café culture. It's all hustle and bustle with a triple mocha frappuccino daily."

"Okay, Neil, if the London Tourist Board need someone, I'll pass on your details,"

"Sorry, guv, but we made more progress through locating Vanessa than any other avenue we'd tried."

"Keep going then. What did Vanessa do for work out of interest?"

"Beauty parlour, would you believe? Her brother had met someone soon after arriving in the city, although Vanessa had never met them. Mark got a call late at night, and she wouldn't see him again until the following evening. So she left for work before Mark returned home."

"Did he talk about this person or the nature of their relationship?"

"Mark never went into details. Vanessa said he was besotted, and the couple planned a future together. Everything came crashing down at the end of February when the affair ended."

"Was he paid for his overnight stays? Did she know where Mark went? What happened to end it?"

"He wouldn't breathe a word, guv, but he was never short of cash. So they went into town shopping every Saturday, and Mark treated Vanessa to clothes, shoes and jewellery. He always dressed smartly."

"So, he arrives here in March 2008, leaving a flashy nightclub in Camden Town for a dead-end job at The Beeches. His lucrative relationship with an unknown person has ended abruptly. He's hurting because he'd believed it was a forever love. When did Vanessa hear from Mark next?"

"That's just it, guv. Mark phoned her dozens of times between March and the end of June. He sounded happy. Suddenly, the calls stopped. She never heard from him for weeks. If she rang his mobile, she got a number unobtainable tone. Then, in August, Vanessa received a postcard from the South of France. The picture on the front was of the promenade at St Tropez. Her address was typed, and there was no scribbled message, just the word 'Heaven' in blue ink."

"Was it in Richards's handwriting?"

"She said it could have been. Unfortunately, he wasn't a great one for writing. Vanessa waited for more news, maybe an invitation to a wedding, a holiday in the Med, but nothing ever came."

"Why didn't she go to the police or try to find him through social media?" asked Lydia.

"London can be a tough place. Vanessa soon struggled financially without Mark to help her, but she's a fighter. Vanessa battled depression and massive debts and came out the other side. Today, she's thirty-two, single, and has her beauty parlour in Camden Town. She told me she prayed every week that Mark was safe and well. In the meantime, she's been grafting eighteen hours a day to keep herself afloat."

Gus leaned back in his chair.

"Right, that's it. We know what happened now. What time is it? I need to check one thing back at HQ. Then I'll brief the Superintendent. He needs to arrange for search warrants."

"Sorry, guv, you've lost us," said Alex.

"It was pretty straightforward. Then, as I drove to Devizes, I realised in the car that Mark Richards was dead. I didn't pass that on to Mercer, of course. Confirmation only came once I'd heard what Neil had to say."

"Will you be back later, guv?" asked Neil, "only it would be nice to know what's going on. So what do we do while you're away?"

"Cancel the meeting with Ricky Edmunds in Swindon. Call Mr Attrill and ask whether they ever saw anyone at Manor House apart from Crompton and Joyce Pemberton-Smythe. Ask Vanessa Richards for Mark's mobile phone number and the name of the nightclub where he worked. I don't think there's anything else. Well, you might tidy this place, gather the paperwork together, and be ready to send it back to HQ. Update the Freeman File with everything you've done today. I'll key in my odds and ends when I return. Well done, and keep up the good work."

With that, he disappeared.

"What the hell was that all about?" asked Alex.

"If Mark Richards is dead," said Lydia, "then the man on the hillside seen by Simon Attrill murdered both him and Daphne Tolliver to stop them from revealing his secret."

"Let's make the calls the boss wants," said Alex.

"Where's a lightbulb moment when you need one," said Neil.

Gus was halfway up the hill out of town by this time. He needed to visit the Hub. He knew something had registered as important when he'd been on the guided tour. Yesterday, he'd realised what it was.

Gus signed in at Reception and told the officer on the desk to ask Geoff Mercer to meet him by the entrance to the Hub. Five minutes later, Geoff came running up to greet him.

"Give me a second to get my breath back, Gus. It sounded urgent; what's up?"

"Let's get inside."

Geoff swiped his card through the scanner, and they entered the Hub. Gus headed straight for the photograph of the opening ceremony.

"As I thought," he said, "the blue phone. Leonard carries it for every personal appearance. Yet on his Westminster office desk, I spotted a white phone. Why have two? Unless one is a prepaid device with a single purpose. To make calls to numbers he doesn't want his family or parliamentary colleagues catching sight of by accident."

"You can't seriously think Leonard Pemberton-Smythe is involved in this matter? Remember what the Chief Constable said. He marked your card only three hours ago."

"Sorry, Geoff, you asked me to be dogged and determined. My team found enough of the missing pieces of the jigsaw for me to see the big picture. Remember the three undisputed facts I told you this morning. First, Simon Attrill was the person in Battersby Lane seen talking to Daphne. Second, a man on the hillside moved away from the murder scene opposite Lowden Park. Third, the other person at the murder scene who ran towards the Park had big feet, and I was convinced that man's name was Mark Richards."

"What did the team uncover while you visited us here at HQ?"

"They traced Vanessa Richards, the running man's sister. She lived with her brother in Camden Town between 2006 and March 2008. He worked as a barman in a nightclub and was having an affair with someone who was married. That person never saw him on a Saturday, so Mark took his sister shopping, spending loads of cash. The fact that this person entertained Mark overnight on any weekday night he chose, suggested it was a hotel or apartment, and the person's actual house was in the country. Mark left home in Kidderminster in 2000 soon after telling his parents he was gay. He worked as a male prostitute in Birmingham and picked up several cautions. Mark moved to London and continued to sell his body. Throughout 2007 there were no cautions or instances of Mark Richards doing anything to alert the police. The sister knew her brother's sexual preferences and didn't feel it necessary to state the lover was male. Mark had come out at sixteen. He was twenty-five in 2008. Who else would he have been in love with?"

"Christ, the shit will hit the fan if you're right."

"I need the warrant to search the grounds of the Manor House for Mark Richards's body. I'll place a bet with you, Geoff. Mark's body lies behind a row of trees, and there will be something in the ground that doesn't belong to him."

"Well, that's easy," groaned Geoff, "I would throw my white phone in the grave I'd dug."

"It's no fun betting with a copper," grinned Gus.

"Do we have sufficient evidence to take before a judge to get a warrant?"

"Let me phone my office. They may have the answer to that by now."

Gus called. Neil answered.

"Did you talk to Mr Attrill?"

"Yes, guv, not sure if it helps, though."

"I'm waiting...."

"He and Simon have visited the Manor House at various times, different weekdays throughout the year since Simon was sixteen. So, they've bumped into gardeners, tree surgeons, plumbers, window cleaners...."

"What about Mr Pemberton-Smythe?"

"Rarely, if ever, guv. Leonard is always away in London. Simon was with his father, chuntering away in the background. His Dad told him to be quiet, but he kept saying the same thing repeatedly."

"Now you see him, now you don't?" asked Gus.

"Blimey, how do you do that, guv?"

"It's a knack, Neil.

"Simon's Dad was about to ring off, and he told me the only time he remembered seeing something odd was soon after Daphne Tolliver's murder. A bloke was walking behind the trees on the far side of the gardens. It was too far away to recognise him. He couldn't work out what he was up to."

"One more thing, Neil, did you find out the nightclub's name?"

"Heaven, guv."

"Of course, thanks, Neil."

Gus clapped his hands.

"OK, Geoff, the body is there behind the trees. Unfortunately, I haven't got a warrant card these days, so you might need to work late tonight. Apologise to Christine on my behalf. I'll have to rearrange my quiet drink with Vera, too, by the looks of it."

"You've asked her out? About time, mate. Good for you. Let me start the ball rolling on this search warrant. We'll get back to my office and head to the Manor House as soon as we get clearance. What put you onto Pemberton-Smythe, anyway?"

"The killer had to be local. That was clear from the outset. They never identified the running man. I wondered whether they had only been in the area briefly before and after the murder. As we picked up pieces of information from Holly Wells, Percy Pickering, the Attrills and the Manor House, I was even more convinced. Simon Attrill couldn't articulate what he meant when he told us he'd seen a man threading his way through the trees on the hillside that evening. Ten years later, that image, reinforced by an image of the same man behind the trees days after the murder, led him to repeat those words to Lydia and me. Now you see him, and now you don't. Simon recognised the man and how he walked through the trees."

"I still don't see how you knew it wasn't an employee. Crompton, perhaps."

"Our MP has his apartment near Russell Square. Vanessa Richards told Neil her brother worked as a barman in a nightclub in Camden Town. A nightclub called 'Heaven' caters to a specific clientele only a ten-minute taxi ride from Russell Square. Leonard and Mark will have met at the end of 2006, and the affair swiftly became monogamous. Leonard was very generous to his lover, hence the weekend shopping sprees. But although Mark believed Leonard would leave Joyce as soon as their sons left school, Leonard had begun to climb the ministerial ladder. He was one of a dozen shadow assistant ministers by February 2008. With the change of Government in May 2010, the opportunity came for his Junior Minister's role at the Home Office. The timing is crucial. Mark had to be ditched because, as a firm believer in family values, Leonard's private life couldn't face scrutiny. Add to that his tough stance on crime. If it had come out that he was bankrolling a male prostitute, it would shatter his credibility. He could forget about the Secretary of State for Justice position, potential Home Secretary and lining himself up for a tilt at the top job."

The phone rang. Geoff answered. Seconds later, he gave Gus the thumbs-up.

"We have your warrant. So let's go," Geoff said, "you can fill me in on the rest on the way."

They descended the stairs and jogged into the car park.

"I'm sold on your reasoning, Gus. God help you if we can't find a body."

"Don't panic, Geoff. Mark Richards told Vanessa several times between March and June how happy he felt. That shows he and Leonard had been in touch. How that happened, we may never know, but Daphne's decision to walk Bobby when and where she did that night proved fatal. The lovers were having sex in the clearing when the old lady disturbed them. Daphne recognises Leonard. Why wouldn't she? He was on her TV as often as he could find a programme to take him. His photograph was everywhere in the Manor House when she did her cleaning. Leonard realised there was no escape. He picked up a rock and smashed her on the head. Mark Richards ran as fast as his legs could carry him. Leonard sneaked home across the hillside after watching Holly discover the body. By that time of night, Joyce was probably drunk. She didn't question him at the best of times. He would have agonised over what to do with Mark. No doubt, he phoned him. On that white phone, telling him to lie low, not speak with anyone, he'd think of something — how, where, and when he killed Mark, we don't know. I suspect Mark would have tried to blackmail him in time. Leonard couldn't take the risk. He killed him within twenty-four hours and buried the body in the grounds of the Manor House in the dead of night. It's a huge area, and the public never visits hundreds of acres of the estate. After he'd done the deed, Simon and his father saw him in the daytime when Leonard made sure he'd hidden the evidence."

"The postcard? I assume you can explain that?" asked Geoff.

"I thought you would have worked that out. It showed a ruthless streak to the Chief Constable's friend, Leonard. We know Joyce and Leonard holiday in France every summer at their chateau. The sons run the family vineyards over there now and rarely visit England. Leonard posted the card from there during that summer's vacation. I doubt Vanessa Richards checked the postmark. To write 'Heaven' in the message space was a cruel touch. Vanessa took it to mean her brother lived with the man he loved, and everything was right with the world, which Leonard intended. The reference to the nightclub where they met merely emphasised that Leonard believed he was in the clear. Nobody would ever discover who killed Daphne Tolliver and Mark Richards."

They were not alone when they arrived at the Manor House. Two vehicles with their crews poised to search the ground for the possible burial site. Geoff Mercer walked up to the door with Gus Freeman and rang the bell.

"This might take some time," said Gus, "the Brazilian cook speaks very little English,"

Maria opened the door. It was clear Geoff's uniform unsettled her. She threw her hands in the air.

Gus had a sudden panic attack. He'd never given a thought to her being illegal.

"Please," she said.

"May I speak with Mrs Pemberton-Smythe, please," Geoff asked.

Joyce Pemberton-Smythe appeared in the doorway. She had been in the conservatory, heard the commotion outside and strolled along to investigate.

"It's alright, Maria, it's that lovely Mr Freeman again. What can we do for you? Oh, someone official. What have we done, pray?"

"Superintendent Mercer, madam, I have a warrant to search the grounds of the Manor House, together with this building, the stables and outbuildings. If you could please remain indoors, I have a family liaison officer who will sit with you. Do you have other staff on the premises?"

Joyce was flustered.

"What on earth are these people doing here? Does the Chief Constable know about this outrage? My husband will return from Westminster within the next two hours. There will be the devil to pay if you are overstepping your powers."

"Understood, madam, but I assure you everything will proceed in line with the warrant issued. I have a copy for you to study. If you wish for another officer to take you through the details, I can supply one. Do you have other staff on the premises?"

"Only Maria and Crompton,"

"Perhaps you could sit with Maria and Crompton and stop him from wandering? Would that be possible?"

"I suppose so. Couldn't Mr Freeman explain this jargon to me?"

"I think Mr Freeman deserves to be involved in the search, madam, as his detective work brought us here. Detective Inspector Ferris is arriving as we speak. She can do the necessary. We'll try not to be too long and keep the disruption to the ground by those trees to an absolute minimum."

Joyce watched as a group of men and women descended from the vehicles and spread out across the lawns leading to the trees in the distance. A smart-looking lady officer climbed the steps and stood next to the Superintendent.

"You had better come in," Joyce said to DI Ferris.

"Good afternoon, madam. Can we make ourselves comfortable somewhere? We may be here for some time. By the way, there will be no incoming or outgoing phone calls until we're finished."

Gus and Geoff left them to it and followed the troops to the tree line.

"Joyce didn't have a clue, did she?" said Geoff.

"Whether she knew about his affair with Mark Richards, or others who came before him, I don't know. Maybe she did but turned a blind eye. But I'm certain she has no idea how far Leonard would go to stop anyone from finding out."

The search began at a quarter past four. The police had three hours of decent daylight.

If they didn't find a body, they'd be back in the morning.

Forty minutes into the probing and digging, there was a shout.

"Got something, Sir."

The other teams paused. Geoff Mercer walked across to see what they had uncovered. Gus followed Geoff, and when they reached the spot, he looked back towards the main building. He could see the line of hanging baskets between the trees gracing the west wing. This place was the one they were after. The scene fitted perfectly with Simon Attrill's image. He breathed a sigh of relief.

Geoff and Gus left the Crime Scene Manager to organise the completion of revealing what lay beneath four feet of soil. The preservation of the scene was paramount. As the two men moved away from the central focus of the operation, they sensed other team members swinging into action. The place would soon be surrounded by 'Police - Do Not Cross' tape. It wouldn't do much to enhance Joyce's view from the conservatory windows, but they had to observe protocols.

When they reached the edge of the lawn, they turned back to watch the well-rehearsed routine unfold. It was a waiting game now. Both men were eager to see what Leonard had wanted to hide for the past ten years, but they would do more harm than good by trying to rush things.

"You were right, Gus. The ACC was right too. You were the best detective to head up this Crime Review Team. At the time it was first mooted, you weren't my first choice, I'll admit. I'm happy to have been proved wrong."

"I'm happy that my first case was so straightforward. As Kierkegaard said, - *Life can only be understood backwards, but it must be lived forwards.* It was easier for me to understand because of the length of time that had elapsed. The young Holly would never have remembered the big white trainers while Culverhouse ran the investigation. It wasn't until she met Danny, her future husband, that a chance remark triggered the memory. We couldn't expect Holly to come forward with that information. She didn't realise its importance. We didn't identify Simon Attrill until Percy Pickering's penchant for collecting indecent images led to him serving a prison sentence. Culverhouse didn't press Pickering on whether he knew the person with Daphne in the lane after he came forward following the reconstruction. Culverhouse had only a general description which didn't produce a response from the Attrills or any locals who could have offered Simon's name as a possibility. Whether Culverhouse would have understood the way Simon described the similarity between the man on the hillside and the man at the Manor House if he'd interviewed him back in 2013, who knows?"

Geoff stared at the ground.

"So, the best way to solve murders might be to leave them for a few years and have another look? That would be popular with the public."

"We'll stick with what we know works most of the time. Our methods won't be completely overhauled because of one success. But, unfortunately, it doesn't always work, Geoff. Think of how many people have tried to find the identity of Jack the Ripper. At last count, it was one of twenty suspects."

"Is there any way Leonard can worm his way out of this?" asked Geoff.

"I'd still like to find the white phone," said Gus, "Mark Richards's phone would be a bonus. Other than that, thanks for reminding me. I meant to ask Neil Davis to call Vanessa Richards. If they were in regular contact, she might have text messages that mention Leonard. Not by name, I suspect, but certainly enough to establish a connection."

A lone figure left the line of trees and walked towards them. There were still signs of activity behind the trees, but the noise wasn't intrusive.

Gus turned and looked back down the driveway to the main gates.

"Thank goodness the Manor House grounds are so extensive. We haven't attracted the attention of the press. No sign of Leonard yet. I wonder how Joyce is coping?"

"Suzie Ferris will keep a lid on things. We can't afford the wife to call Leonard and tip him off. We'll arrest him when he gets home. There was no point racing up to the Palace of Westminster. We'd never avoid alerting the media then."

"I thought it might take longer to get this case sorted," said Gus. "When we were with the Chief Constable this morning, I wondered what his reaction would be if we turned up on the first tee at North Wilts on Sunday morning and took his chum away on two counts of murder. As it is, we should be able to give him time to ring around for a replacement."

"You're all heart, Freeman," said Geoff. "No matter how delicately we negotiate the next few hours, there will be a major shitstorm when this story breaks. The county boundaries won't contain the blast area. This story will receive national headlines for days. Our Chief Constable may have more to worry about than his golf foursomes. Once their friendship becomes public, he'll be lucky to survive."

Gus shrugged.

"I'm not concerned with the fallout this case brings. I was only interested in finally catching Daphne Tolliver's killer."

The Police Surgeon approached Geoff Mercer. He looked the same age as Gus, with a demeanour that suggested 'world-weary'.

"You picked a fine time to call me out, the last thing on a Friday afternoon. I had hoped to be on the motorway already heading for a weekend in the Brecon Beacons.

"I'm sorry, Peter. Have you ever met Gus Freeman? He was a DI in the Salisbury area until a few years back. Gus, this is Peter Morgan. He's one of the best police surgeons I've had the misfortune to work with."

"Many thanks for sparing the time to help us out. Peter," said Gus.

"I'd shake your hand, Gus, but I don't have one free," he replied, waving two evidence bags. "The CSM thought you would be interested in my initial findings and what we found amongst the skeletal remains."

Gus and Geoff grabbed a bag each.

"We have an adult male in the ground behind the trees. The body's condition indicates he has been there between eight and twelve years. The skull suffered damage in the right parietal lobe region. I guess someone bashed him over the head with a blunt object. Also, I found these mobile phones beneath the feet. I'll be able to tell you more once my examinations are complete."

"Thanks, Peter. How long before they can get everything out and back to the morgue?"

"Another two hours, at least, I should say. They don't need me for that. I'll make tracks. I might get across the Bridge before the traffic gets too hectic."

Peter Morgan strode off to a Porsche Boxster parked between two police vans.

"We're in the wrong job," said Geoff, "now, are these the two missing phones?"

"I grabbed the white one as soon as I saw it," said Gus. "We need to get both tested to see how much can be retrieved and match it to the one Leonard had on his desk in his office at Westminster."

"If this red phone is Mark Richards's, then we must hope we can retrieve messages received from Leonard. Of course, his sister can confirm if he owned a phone like this, but getting something useful from it will strengthen our case."

"Your people in the Hub will be our best bet. Don't try turning these on. Even deleted text messages sit there until overwritten. If we poke around, we might overwrite something that would prove damning. We must leave this to the experts."

"Agreed," said Geoff, "let's return these to the Exhibits Officer. I'll arrange a welcoming party for Pemberton-Smythe. We'll get a car to park on the approach road, and then they can tail him to the gates. If he tries to escape, we'll get the road blocked around the bend, two hundred yards past the entrance. So his visibility will be negligible. As long as we're sensible, we won't spook him."

"I think you've got everything covered," said Gus, "I'll make a few calls."

"Say hello from me," Geoff called as Gus moved away to the other side of the House's front steps.

Gus rang the office first. It was after five o'clock. He didn't know whether they would have stayed. Neil answered.

"All good," said Gus, "we found the body where I predicted. Pemberton-Smythe buried two mobile phones in the grave along with Mark Richards. I'm confident tests will show one belonged to Richards, and the other was the single-use white phone the politician used exclusively to call his lover."

"When will you make an arrest, guv?"

"Superintendent Mercer will arrest the culprit in the next ninety minutes."

"Time for a celebration, guv,"

"If you can make it to the Waggon & Horses in Harrington End by nine tonight, you'll find I'm in the chair. Not just for the first round either."

"Wild horses, guv. We'll be there."

Gus ended the call and then rang Vera.

"Hi," she said, "don't tell me you're standing me up?"

"I wouldn't dare. But, look, it might not be a quiet drink later. I've invited the team to join us to celebrate our success. Geoff Mercer will arrest a double killer before long."

"You didn't meet the team until Monday morning. You were hoping to solve one murder. Instead, by Friday, you've uncovered and solved a second. Gus Freeman, you are a magician."

"See you at nine," said Gus.

His last call was to the ACC. Kenneth Truelove sat at home waiting for news on the operation.

"Truelove, here,"

"Good evening, Sir. It's Gus Freeman here. I won't steal Geoff Mercer's thunder. He can fill you in later. You may want to get to the town's custody suite to watch the proceedings. The cells will have an important guest shortly. Unfortunately, we need to notify a family in Kidderminster and a sister in Camden Town of a death. I should notify the sister tomorrow if that's in order. Neil Davis can accompany me. The man's parents can be informed by the local police, although I doubt it will worry them one way or another."

"Whatever you say, Freeman. How can I refuse? An incredible week. Incredible."

"Please don't think this will be a regular occurrence, Sir. I understand you have other cases you wish us to review. Perhaps, I can call in on Monday morning to pick up the details of the next one?"

"Certainly, Freeman. Thank you for ringing."

Gus looked up at the imposing Manor House. It loomed over him as dusk fell. In the distance, he could see lights and a white tent over the gravesite. Geoff Mercer's men wheeled the stretcher carrying Mark Richards's body to a van. The transfer was timed to coincide with the arrival of the local Member of Parliament.

The cars would be in the position now, and the trap set.

CHAPTER 12

Gus watched as the lights of the Jaguar pierced the gloom.

The tail car waited outside the gates while the vans removing the body and items of evidence edged along the driveway. The Jaguar slowed too, its driver perhaps realising the significance of their contents.

Leonard Pemberton-Smythe's car halted fifty yards from the bottom of the steps. The vehicles from the proposed blockade now occupied the throat of the entrance beside the tail car. There was no escape.

Geoff Mercer and another DI strode forward. Uniformed officers approached the car but stood five yards away. The cordon was secure. The driver's door opened, and Leonard Pemberton-Smythe got out.

A tall man solidly built. Many pundits described Pemberton-Smythe as 'imposing' when speaking in the House of Commons. Gus watched as he slid his briefcase from the rear near-side passenger seat and locked the car with a flourish of his remote key. He did not comment. He walked to where Geoff stood and stopped.

"Mercer, isn't it? I remember you from Devizes HQ. I'm calling a lawyer if you wish to continue this pantomime."

"Leonard Pemberton-Smythe, you are being arrested in connection with the murder of Daphne Tolliver on the twenty-eighth of June 2008 and Mark Richards between the twenty-eighth of June and the third of July 2008. You have the right to remain silent. If you say anything, what you say can be used against you in a court of law. You have the right to consult with a lawyer and have that lawyer present during any questioning. If you cannot afford a lawyer, one will be appointed for you if you so desire. We will take you to the custody suite on the outskirts of town.

You'll remember where that is. You were present at that opening ceremony too. You can contact your lawyer then. Do you wish to inform anyone else of what's happening to you, Sir?"

"Tell my wife to expect me home for supper."

"We'd not want to raise her hopes, Sir, but we will tell her where you will go for questioning."

Gus wished Geoff Mercer was taller; his neck must hurt after looking up for so long. He watched as officers led the prisoner to Geoff's car. How the mighty were fallen. He kept going over the facts they had uncovered, testing each for a weakness, wondering how an expensive QC might approach the interview. They had twenty-four hours.

Time was short. Much of their evidence might be circumstantial, but Gus had just spotted another thing that pointed the finger at Pemberton-Smythe.

One by one, the cars left the car park. Finally, Gus climbed the steps to the front door and rang the bell. Maria answered.

She stood to the side to allow him in but didn't say a word. DI Ferris stood in the hallway with Joyce. Crompton had presumably stayed in his quarters.

"I've told Mrs Pemberton-Smythe where her husband is going and why," she said, "my job here is over. Can I give you a lift anywhere?"

"My car is in the London Road car park. Geoff ferried me over. He didn't have room on his next trip."

"It's on my way home. Shall we?"

"I'm sorry about this business," Gus said to Joyce.

"I'm sure it will be over before bedtime," she said.

Gus could see she was heartbroken. A brave face was a poor substitute for a suit of armour. Joyce needed that and more in the coming weeks. He feared another stint in The Priory lay ahead.

When they reached London road, Suzie Ferris dropped him by his car.

"A Ford Focus," she said, "my Dad had one of those. Steady little runner. Have a good weekend. You've earned a break."

With that, she drove away.

"Don't worry, she didn't mean you were old," he patted the car's roof before he got in to drive home to Urchfont.

Friday nights in the Waggon & Horses were lively affairs. Good food in the restaurant. A band was rocking out covers from the Eighties and Nineties in the Stable Bar. When Gus arrived, there were a few parking spaces left. Some stood on the grass verges on either side of the pub. It would lead to problems later, but he risked his Ford Focus. Another dent wouldn't matter that much.

Gus peered through the windows of the Stable Bar. A younger crowd. The band was loud — not his cup of tea. Perhaps sixty people were being served various dishes in the restaurant — still no familiar faces. In the far corner was a smaller bar that had to be for the non-eaters and non-rockers. That looked busy too.

Neil, Alex and Lydia were at least one drink ahead of him. There was no sign of Vera Jennings. He scoured the bar and checked his watch; it was only nine o'clock. Lydia was soon by his side.

"If you're buying, guv, we've started a tab under the name Freeman. So we'll have the same again. What a result. It took us a while to get our heads around your logic."

"Please tell me you didn't find any flaws?"

"Alex thought it was very Poirot-like the way you unravelled it. But, gosh, don't look now, guv, but there's a heart attack in a dress behind you."

Gus turned around.

"Vera, glad you could make it. Come and meet the team."

The following two hours flew past. Vera and Gus ensured the conversation was a million miles away from work. Lydia persuaded Alex to let her wheel him in to listen to the band. Neil looked at the near-empty glass before him and weighed up buying another against Gus's announcement they were off to London in the morning.

"That's me done," he said. "I'll ring Melody to come to fetch me. She'll be surprised it's early, and I'm not pissed, but needs must."

"I'll swing by and pick you up at half-past eight, Neil," Gus told him.

"Alone at last," said Gus, twenty minutes later, as Neil trotted outside to hop in his wife's car.

"Not for long, I'm going too," said Vera. "This has been fun. We should do something again. Maybe come out here for a meal."

Gus settled the bar tab and followed Vera out to her car. It was in a wide parking space in the car park.

"Too dangerous on the verges," she said.

They stopped by the driver's door.

Gus wasn't sure whether to make a move. He felt sixteen again.

Vera leaned forward and kissed him on the lips. It felt good. They both heard the squeal of brakes and a metallic crunch.

"Told you," she said, squeezing his hand as she got into the Alfa Romeo, "Sweet dreams."

"I wish she wouldn't say that," Gus thought as she pulled into the lane and drove away. He trudged along the row of parked cars, dreading the worst. A Honda Jazz had parked one space beyond the Focus, facing towards him. They'd reversed into the lane just as an ancient Defender rounded the corner. The rear of the Jazz was not a pretty sight. He moved his Focus carefully out onto the lane and drove home. It wasn't his place to get involved these days. His luck had changed.

Sweet dreams.

Saturday, 14th April 2018

Gus collected Neil from home and made it to London before ten o'clock. Reaching Camden Town wasn't as difficult as it might have been on a weekday. But, unfortunately, a parking place was crazy difficult to find as always.

Saturday was a busy day at Vanessa Richards's beauty parlour. The receptionist told them Miss Vanessa was fully booked with clients today. However, one of their other beauticians would be free if they wished to wait. Gus Freeman told her he wasn't looking for a pedicure or Botox, and he and Neil waved cards under her pert little nose.

"A Saturday girl," said Neil, "only looks thirteen."

Vanessa Richards appeared from behind a screen.

"DS Davis, we spoke on the phone," said Neil.

Vanessa's face crumpled as soon as she realised why they had turned up in person.

"No!" she wailed, "not Mark? He was so happy."

"Let's go through to the back of the shop, Miss Richards," said Gus, "to give you a little privacy."

Gus told her they found a body. He asked if she could describe his mobile phone. The make and model were identical, and Vanessa confirmed it was red. Gus told her they had found it with the body. He said Mark's murder had occurred only hours or a few days after the murder of a woman in Wiltshire. The same man was responsible. That man had been Mark's mysterious lover.

"But the postcard," Vanessa cried.

"Do you still have it?" asked Neil.

"It's at home, in my flat."

"We'd like to borrow it if we may. We need to enter it into evidence."

Gus asked her to show him her mobile phone.

"Could you give me Mark's number, please?"

Vanessa scrolled through her contacts and showed Gus the number. He made a note of it.

"Would you have kept any text messages from your brother? I know it was long ago, and you've probably changed phones and suppliers a dozen times since then...."

"Yeah, I've got all his old messages. I always hoped he'd get in touch again. So I move the ones I want to keep from the old phone to the new one using Bluetooth. It's dead simple."

It might be for you, Gus thought. He could have kissed her.

"Do you have an example?" he asked.

"How about this one," she said, scrolling through until she found the one she wanted.

"This one's from early in 2007." She read it from the screen: -

He has a nice car, collects me, and then drives me to his flat. He has a house in the country but uses the place in London for his liaisons. He's married, but they don't have much of a relationship. He's a politician. He didn't think I knew who he was when we met, but I'm not stupid. I watch the News, Question Time and Have I Got News for You.

"Mark doesn't name him, guv," said Neil.

"This isn't the only SMS, Neil. I doubt we'll find a name, but this is more than enough on top of everything else. Now, if we can work out how to capture these messages onto one of our phones...."

"Give it here. I'll do it," said Vanessa.

"Do you have anybody to be with you?" asked Neil, "you've had a shock. Perhaps we should take you home, pick up that postcard and then give you details of what will happen next. We've contacted your parents. I don't know what their reaction will be. Funeral arrangements and so on."

"I'll look after him if they ignore him. I never stopped loving him. We are what we are. I'm not seeing anyone right now, but I'll be okay. You're right. I'll apologise to my clients and pass them on to the others. I need time alone."

Gus and Neil left Vanessa Richards in her apartment in the middle of the afternoon. Gus had listened as she talked of the Mark she knew as a child. She showed them pictures of her brother until he was sixteen.

"Mark left home, and there weren't any family ones after that. I've got a few on my phone taken at birthdays or Christmas of just me and him here in London. He was always self-conscious of having his picture taken."

"Big feet?" asked Neil.

Vanessa looked at him in amazement.

"How the heck did you know that? He was only size ten, but his build was more like a young girl's. When he had a pair of trainers, they looked like a couple of boats. Especially white ones."

Neil Davis turned to his boss as they sped along the M4 on the return journey.

"How will the interview have gone so far, do you think, guv?"

"I'm not worried about the outcome," said Gus, "we've got enough to hold him beyond the twenty-four hours. What we've picked up today are more pieces of the jigsaw. The text messages are damning. The postcard could contain his fingerprints. French and British postal service personnel will have handled it. After that, only Vanessa Richards touched it without gloves. If Leonard doesn't confess, then we can get the handwriting analysed. We can look for the equipment he used to type the address at the chateau. The fact it was posted less than half a mile from the Pemberton-Smythe's holiday home will be hard to explain. Leonard showered Mark with bundles of cash, according to Vanessa. The Hub can home in on that aspect. Frequent significant sums should be withdrawn throughout 2007 and the following year. No, I'm not worried. Other witnesses placed Leonard in the cell, and Vanessa started turning the key in the lock."

They arrived at Neil's house just before five.

"See you Monday morning then, guv," he said.

"New week, new case," said Gus.

"We've got a load more work to do on this one yet, guv."

"I intend to pass these enquiries on to Geoff Mercer and his real-time detective team. The Hub will handle most tasks. Our job was to find the killer, and we did that. So they can prepare the case to take it to court. The more evidence they can pile in front of Leonard and his QC, the easier things will be."

"Fair enough," said Neil, "let this be our motto - Another Day, Another Collar."

Gus drove away. Another day, another collar; it had a ring to it.

He parked the Focus in its usual spot to the right of the bungalow and went indoors. Time for a shower, then change into casual clothing and decide what to eat. He could pay a visit to the allotment before night fell.

The phone rang. Gus looked at the number; it looked familiar.

"Mr Freeman, it's Joyce Pemberton-Smythe here."

"If you're wondering what's happening with your husband, I can't tell you anything. I've passed responsibility over to Superintendent Mercer. As I explained on our first visit to the Manor House, I'm a mere consultant, not a serving officer."

"You made that crystal clear," she said, "I wanted you to know the diaries I referred to still exist. Since your people took Leonard away, I've sat here wondering what point there was denying you the chance to see them."

"I can be there in twenty minutes."

Thoughts of a visit to the allotment were on hold. Instead, Gus raced to the Manor House. Joyce met him at the door and showed him into one of the drawing rooms.

"I hid them in the chest of drawers. Leonard never came into this room. The diary for the end of June is open at the relevant entries."

It appeared Leonard caught a chill in a heavy downpour on Saturday evening. As a result, he didn't rush back to London on Sunday night. Instead, he slept in on Monday and lazed around until lunchtime. Then, he was out for the rest of the day. Joyce didn't see him again until breakfast on Tuesday morning. 'Leonard is still under the weather.' The first entry on Wednesday the second of July was 'Left for the House before dawn'.

"May I take this diary?" he asked.

"You will be discreet, won't you? You promised."

"I'm the soul of discretion. So we will only use the elements that strengthen our case."

"Crompton can confirm the events of those few days."

Gus thought that highly unlikely.

"I can see you doubt me," said Joyce, "walk this way."

Crompton sat in the window seat, dressed as he had been the other morning.

"Don't get up," said Joyce, moving swiftly to the desk. She retrieved a book from a drawer.

"Look familiar? Every year, I gave the staff a diary to record our comings and goings when tradespeople were due. Crompton used his diary for extra items. Here, you can see listed the meal served each day. He said it helped him maintain variety. For example, on Monday, he cooked a pork loin for us. On Tuesday, Leonard was out, so Crompton reverted to what was typical when he stayed in London."

Gus could read 'Light supper' and 'ditto' for Wednesday and Thursday.

"Easy to understand why I ate so little. I drank heavily back then. To sit at a table for a three-course meal kept me from the vodka bottle for far too long."

Gus wondered how the stress of yesterday's events would affect Joyce's mental health. Joyce had come so far that it would be a tragedy if she fell off the wagon now.

"I should like to borrow this too, if I may," he said.

"Crompton won't mind, I'm sure."

Joyce walked Gus to the door.

"The next few weeks will be tough," she said, "but I can only try to take them one day at a time. DI Ferris talked to me yesterday about the charges against my husband. I knew he was bi-sexual when we married. He kept his other side hidden, so the boys and I were protected. It was easier to pretend it wasn't an issue. What happened in London stayed in London. After you left with DI Ferris yesterday, I reflected on that weekend and the following days. I checked the diary before I rang you. We were collecting the boys from boarding school on the fourth of July. This man, Richards, must have given Leonard an ultimatum. Tell your wife, or I'll go to the police about poor old Daffers. That's why Leonard felt he had to kill him. We were bound for the chateau on the ferry on Friday evening."

"These diaries will help complete the prosecution case, madam. I'm very grateful. Leonard's actions have caused pain to so many people. The woman I saw caring for Crompton the other day deserved better. Good luck."

Gus drove away and saw Joyce leaning against the open front door until he passed through the gates. He hoped her sons were on their way home to comfort her.

It was certain Leonard continued his liaisons after Mark Richards was dead. They had to hope none became so serious that such extreme measures ensued. Gus wondered whether he took time off when he holidayed in France. What a mess. The number of young men who might come forward to sell their stories to the press would fill the media for years. Poor Joyce and her sons would never escape.

As he drove into town, he thought it was time he called on Megan and Mick Morris. They needed to hear someone had been arrested for Daphne's murder before the press picked up the story. One more small job before getting home. The allotment would have to wait until the morning.

Monday would come around soon enough. His first port of call then was London Road and a briefing with the ACC.

Life is not a problem to be solved but a reality to experience.

Gus Freeman wondered what experiences lay ahead on their next cold case.

You have just finished reading 'Fatal Decision.'

The first book in the series featuring **'The Freeman Files'**.

Why not read the first chapter of **'Last Orders'**, the second book in the series?

CHAPTER 1

Sunday 15th April 2018

The best-laid plans can often go astray.

Gus Freeman woke early and showered and dressed before eight o'clock. Then, finally, he stood ready for the day ahead. A glance through his kitchen window confirmed the weather remained cloudy but mild.

As the clock ticked around to the top of the hour, he decided on healthy oats and yoghurt for breakfast. Those suit trousers in his wardrobe only had one waistband extender button, and he'd already taken advantage of that. There would be plenty of opportunities to check out the other taste sensations amassed in his storage units.

Gus had restocked his fridge and freezer ahead of weeks, searching through a maze of questions posed by the ten-year-old murder of Mrs Daphne Tolliver. Finally, after three years of retirement, he returned to the job he had performed successfully for forty years. Gus Freeman merited his reputation as an excellent detective.

Assistant Chief Constable Kenneth Truelove persuaded him half a dozen cold cases had his name on them. Then, in a moment of weakness, perhaps blinded by the beauty of the ACC's PA, Vera Jennings, Gus put aside his gardening tools and re-entered the fray.

In his absence, the ongoing fight against crime had become an even more uphill battle. Cuts in the number of front-line officers were the most visible evidence to those who suffered as a result. Austerity cut deeper wounds in support staff, too; the police service that faced Gus on his return was lower on morale than when he retired. Something he didn't believe was possible.

Gus reflected on the speed of events in the past week. The knack for asking the right questions of the right people paid dividends. The old methods proved helpful yet again.

Even though he had only met his Crime Review Team members on Monday morning, they unmasked the killer by late Friday afternoon. Detective Superintendent Geoff Mercer arrested Leonard Pemberton-Smythe, the local MP, in front of the Manor House, the imposing country pile Leonard shared with his wife, Joyce and their staff.

Pemberton-Smythe was touted as the next Home Secretary and shortlisted for the highest office in the land. Gus and his team examined events surrounding the evening of Saturday, the twenty-eighth of June 2008. They discovered that the disgraced politician had committed not one murder but two.

Gus spooned the last of his breakfast from the bowl. He grimaced as he swallowed the healthy concoction. First things first, he popped into the bedroom to set the alarm for the following morning. Even if it meant forgoing fifteen minutes in bed, fried egg, bacon, and sausage was a better start to the day. Why support the producers of Scottish oats and Greek yoghurts when he could find locally sourced fresh food from farms within three miles?

If the worst came to the worst, he could always drive into town after meeting with the ACC in the morning and get a new suit.

Yesterday had been a busy day. He and Neil Davis, one of his two Detective Sergeants on the team, drove to London to interview Vanessa, the sister of the second victim, Mark Richards. Richards and Pemberton-Smythe were lovers. A relationship that proved fatal for the younger man when Daphne Tolliver disturbed the two men in Lowden Woods.

The old lady had to die to protect the Secretary of State for Justice's reputation. Richards died because he was a witness. The volatile nature of the relationship convinced the

MP that two deaths were more acceptable than leaving himself open to blackmail.

Gus returned from the capital with vital information to strengthen the case against Pemberton-Smythe. An early evening visit to the Manor House produced more damning documentation from the MP's wife, Joyce. Gus could add that to the impressive pile of evidence for the prosecution later this morning.

It had been a grand day out. Even the sad duty of calling on Megan and Mick Morris felt cathartic. Gus told them they had closed Megan's sister's case at last. They had arrested her killer. Gus sat with them for over an hour, hoping the news might bring them closure, but the truth was far worse than they imagined. The killer was someone they knew. An important person in the public eye killed two innocent people. Daphne had worked at the Manor House for six years. It was hard for them to comprehend.

Gus knew there would be shock and dismay when the news reached the media. There would be disbelief and questions asked. Had the police got the right man? Could Wiltshire Police run as sensitive an investigation as this? Who was in charge? He was thankful the buck stopped with the ACC and Geoff Mercer. Those two had broad shoulders. But, one thing was guaranteed; the Corporate Communications and Engagement people would earn their crust in the coming days.

Gus was one hundred per cent sure that the man DS Mercer would interview again later this morning was guilty. Two counts of murder. Bang to rights. It was time for the Crime Review Team to move on to its next case.

Gus gathered the documentation and his phone with the messages Vanessa had kept for a decade and left the bungalow despite the early hour. He locked the items in his Ford Focus glove compartment and drove through Urchfont village to the allotments. Ten minutes spent catching up on how his plants were coping wouldn't put a significant dent in his day.

There was no sign of Bert Penman. He'd be working here this afternoon after attending morning service at the church up the road. The bells hadn't started to ring yet. The silence on a morning such as this was a blessing. Few cars were on the road, and the birds grasped the opportunity to fill the temporary gap. Gus sat outside his shed for a spell.

He enjoyed two minutes alone with his thoughts.

"Mr Freeman?"

Irene North, Frank's wife, arrived beside him. Gus thought she could work for the SAS; he hadn't heard a sound.

"Good morning, Mrs North," he said.

"Frank hasn't been home," said Irene.

Gus gave her his full attention. Irene North was not trying to catch Frank smoking a crafty ciggy. Nevertheless, the deep concern on a face lined with age and the worry of being married to a habitual offender was genuine. Gus had a terrible thought.

"When did you last see him, Mrs North?"

"Frank said he was coming here last night to check he'd locked his shed. He reckoned he was gardening for four hours yesterday afternoon. Frank spent it smoking and chatting, I'll bet. Don't think I don't know what he gets up to when he's here. I wouldn't mind if he brought armfuls of fruit and vegetables home, but Frank's got light fingers, not green."

"So I understand, Mrs North. He assures me that's in the past, though, and he's mended his ways. I couldn't get to my allotment yesterday, so I can't confirm if he was here. Frank's shed is locked, as you can see. What time did he leave home?"

"Just before ten,"

"Did he wear a coat, carry a torch? Did he go prepared?

"Frank didn't go out late at night without a hat and coat, not with the state of his chest. I don't know if he took a torch. Knowing him, he'd strike a match to see whether that lock was secure. Then he'd just as likely light a blessed fag with it so as not to waste the match."

Gus understood Irene North's concern. Both were in their seventies and stayed together through thick and thin. Frank was as skinny as a rake. His long-suffering wife made three of him. Irene might give her old man a hard time over his smoking, but a deep affection was involved if their marriage had survived this long. Even if it lay hidden.

Gus considered the situation. Frank North was old, not in the best of health, and missing for twelve hours. He knew Frank could have been taken ill or had fallen in the dark and lay hurt somewhere. But he and Irene walked past the likely spots when they came to the allotments. There was just one road through the village. Frank and Irene's place stood four hundred yards away.

So, where else might he have gone? Ah, the glorified shed belonging to Monty Jennings, Vera's estranged husband.

Geoff Mercer had told Gus that initial surveillance of the land behind Cambrai Terrace began last night. Plain-clothes officers had watched the lane entrance for strangers. The plan was to gather information to add weight to Frank's argument someone was living there. If people were living on the property, then that posed a problem. Nobody had ever applied for planning permission.

Gus told Frank not to stick his nose into the matter after he'd passed the issue on to the proper authorities. What if the silly old sod ignored his warning and wandered along the lane behind Cambrai Terrace for a quick peek? The officers on watch would have thought he was up to his old tricks with his reputation. Frank North was housebreaking yet again. Irene's best chance of finding her husband might be at the local police station.

"I don't think you need to fret over Frank," said Gus. "If he'd had a stroke or tripped and broken a hip, we would have found him somewhere between your home and here. Telephone the police. If he's wandered off somewhere, they could keep an eye out. He's had his moments. Although he swore to me that he'd stopped the thieving nonsense. We must accept he might have lapsed. In which case, the police could have him."

"I'll swing for him if that's what he was up to last night."

"At least you'll know where he is, Mrs North," said Gus.

Despite the potential seriousness of the situation, Irene North treated Gus to a gap-toothed smile. However, she soon returned to her standard disparaging tone.

"He can kiss goodbye to me visiting him this time," she said. "Our pensions barely put food on the table. There won't be spare cash for half-hour bus trips to Erlestoke."

With that, Irene North made her way home. Gus gave up working on his allotment. He relied on Bert Penman to sort out any urgent problems. The sooner he got the evidence he collected yesterday to Geoff Mercer, the better.

The trip into the valley was a pleasant one. Everything was coming together. The sun shone, and their first case went well. Alex, Neil and Lydia had the makings of an effective team. He'd taken the first step towards having a social life again with Vera Jennings. Where it might lead, Gus didn't have a clue.

He swung his Ford Focus into an empty parking spot outside the new custody suite on the outskirts of town. Gus was coming to terms with the layout of his new working environment. He welcomed the opportunity to see inside this modern addition to the Wiltshire Police family. The compound held several Bobby Vans and signs that the Neighbourhood Policing Units were well-represented. Even on a Sunday morning, there was a buzz about the place. But, of course, it may have been a swarm of flies or a dodgy streetlight.

Once inside the building, he asked to speak with Superintendent Mercer.

"The DS is interviewing a suspect at present. Perhaps if you take a seat?"

"I suggest you get a message to him," said Gus, "the items I have here are evidence. He should have enough for a result, but if the suspect's lawyer still retains a faint hope, this should shatter any illusions of a miracle."

Gus only needed to wait five minutes. Then, Geoff Mercer came out to greet him.

"Good to see you, Gus," he said. "That QC he's engaged is keeping us on our toes. We're well ahead on points, though. Another session, and they should see sense and throw in the towel."

"I bear good tidings," said Gus, "we have text message conversations between Mark and Vanessa Richards from 2007 that confirm he was in a relationship with a senior politician. We have details of the location of the Minister's apartment. We identified the nightclub where they first met. There's a postcard sent to the sister from the village where Pemberton-Smythe had his holiday home. Mark was supposed to have sent it, but he was already dead and buried in the grounds of the Manor House. An expert can examine the handwriting, if necessary."

"This is dynamite, Gus, thanks," said Geoff. "I want to listen to these messages before I go back. They asked for a fifteen-minute comfort break. I plan to be lenient on timekeeping. It will suggest we're on the run. The impact of this additional evidence will be even greater. What else do you have there?"

"Joyce Pemberton-Smythe produced diary details of Leonard's activities on the Saturday evening of the murder. Based on entries in both Joyce and Crompton's diaries, he was not at home. Although he *was* out in the rain long enough to catch a chill, he delayed his return to Westminster until early on Wednesday morning. That was a complete change of routine. It was unique, based on the evidence in the diaries. He left the house at lunchtime on Monday and didn't return until after Joyce went to bed. The murder and the subsequent burial of the body took place during those missing hours."

"This will help speed matters," said Geoff, rubbing his hands in anticipation. "Many thanks for this, Gus. I'll get these items processed. Do you want to observe? There's a spare chair next to Interview Room One."

"I'm not bothered," said Gus, "I can leave things in your capable hands. Even you couldn't fail to score from this distance."

"I knew you hadn't changed, deep down, you bugger."

"Did the surveillance crew spot anything or anyone last night?"

"Ah, sorry," said Geoff, "we pulled so many resources out to the Manor House that we left ourselves stretched. Then there was an incident on the M4 between Chippenham and Bath. A youngster jumped from a bridge. So we postponed the whole thing. I've been too busy here to organise another try."

"Damn," said Gus, "I may need to look up there myself."

"The shed's not going anywhere; surely whatever Monty's involved in can wait?"

"Frank North is missing. He's the old chap who first gave me this tip. He's got the patch next to me on the allotments. His wife told me this morning that Frank left home at ten last night and never returned."

"Look, I need to get back inside with this evidence," said Geoff. "Call Suzie Ferris. The counter staff will give you her number after I've convinced them you're one of the good guys. Go with her to see what's what. Then, if it needs an official investigation, Suzie can start the ball rolling."

Gus nodded. He watched Geoff Mercer pause at the desk as he rushed through to carry on the interview with Pemberton-Smythe and the expensive QC he'd called. In the old days, Gus would have driven up to Cambrai Terrace, nosed around and thought nothing of nicking a suspect if he uncovered criminal activity. Instead, as a consultant, he needed a serving officer to help him do even the basics.

That was the negative side of things. Suzie Ferris was young, attractive and on a fast track to the top. He could think of worse ways to spend a Sunday afternoon.

The young constable on the counter handed over Suzie's number, and Gus entered it into his phone. His contact list was growing apace after three years of inactivity.

"Suzie?" he asked, "Gus Freeman here. Sorry to bother you on Sunday morning. Can you spare an hour?"

"I didn't expect to hear from you, Gus. I told you to put your feet up and relax. Re-charge the batteries after a busy week."

Gus wondered why Suzie imagined he needed a long bed rest after spending a few days in the office. He was only sixty-one, for heaven's sake.

"Geoff Mercer is interviewing our man here at the custody suite. He volunteered your services. How long will it take you to get to Urchfont?"

"Fifteen minutes," replied Suzie, "isn't that where you live?"

Gus sensed another question left unasked.

"I live in the village, but that's not where Geoff volunteered your services. It's above board. We're searching for a missing person, so I'll fill you in when I get there. I'm leaving the police station now, and we'll meet at the end of Cambrai Terrace. It's on a hillside at the edge of the village."

"I've ridden past there," said Suzie, "the lanes there aren't ideal for hacking, but it's a light exercise for my horses and good relaxation for me. Drive safe."

Gus wasn't surprised to learn Suzie was a horsewoman. There were plenty of them in the area. The Avon Vale branch of the Pony Club was on her doorstep. Her accent wasn't broad enough to place her as Wiltshire, born and bred. If she grew up near Devizes, her love of horses probably started before she went to school.

"Drive safe, indeed," he muttered as he left the custody suite and drove along Crook Way. He hadn't forgotten her unmerited swipe at his elderly Ford Focus on Friday evening. Suzie was waiting in her Golf GTI in a passing place on what amounted to little more than a single-track road.

Typical, she must have broken the speed limit to arrive ahead of me, thought Gus.

Suzie watched Gus park, then got out and walked towards his car.

Gus had admired the smart-looking officer in her uniform at the Manor House. Today Suzie's hair hung loose on her shoulders, not pinned in a bun under her hat. Her black blouson jacket covered a navy-blue polo shirt. Jodhpurs and riding boots completed the outfit of a girl at home in the country.

"Where are we off to?" she asked.

"Let's stroll along Cambrai Terrace, to begin with," he said, "I'll bring you up to speed on the story so far. We're interested in anything beyond the houses rather than the houses themselves. I hope we can tell whether anyone is hanging around in the fields above us on this first recce. It might be dangerous to get too close."

"You didn't tell me this might be dangerous," said Suzie. "It's okay; I carry my expanding baton and pepper spray in the car. I'll pick it up when we walk back. That's why we girls carry these huge handbags. I bet you thought it was just because they were trendy."

As they strolled along Cambrai Terrace, Gus told Suzie of the strange goings-on Frank North had reported. Her eyebrows shot up when he mentioned Monty Jennings owned the land which contained the glorified shed.

"So, this poor old chap has been missing since late last night? What would they do if something illegal was happening on the premises and he stumbled on it?"

"That's exactly why I told Frank to stay away," said Gus. "Monty Jennings flies close to the wind, according to Geoff Mercer. Violence doesn't appear to be in his make-up."

"He may have leased the place to someone else," said Suzie, glancing over Gus's shoulder as they turned into the cul-de-sac at the end of the road.

"I couldn't see anyone," said Gus, "how about you? Any sign of smoke?"

"Nothing at all. We can't be sure there aren't vehicles in the lane behind the houses. We'd have a better view if we walked up to the brow of the hill and cut across the field. It won't attract as much attention if we pose as ramblers looking across the valley."

"Smart move, dressing the way you did. You blend into the scenery."

"You decided on smart-casual this time."

Her laughter was infectious.

Gus realised she'd learned about his first meeting with the ACC. So, after three years of dressing as he pleased and spending most of his spare time on his allotment, he drove to the London Road HQ in his gardening clothes.

Suzie trotted ahead of him to collect her baton and pepper spray from the boot of her car. She dropped the items into her shoulder bag, together with her warrant card. Suzie paused as she passed the strap of her handbag over her head to prevent it from being ripped from her by an attacker.

"There's no telling to whom Monty might have leased this place," she said, "Vera says he'll do anything to make a quick profit."

"That worried me too," said Gus, "we've got three sizeable cities within twenty miles. County lines gangs have been growing in strength and numbers. If they're involved in this, Frank North could have walked into a heap of trouble."

The winding lane took them ever upward to the brow of the hill and disappeared into the valley. From the ridge, they could see the lane running along the backs of the houses on

Cambrai Terrace. At the far end stood the outbuilding. It was too substantial to call it a shed. The chimney was only an ornament today, but why would anyone need to add a chimney to a property designed to store tools and equipment? A vast expanse of greenery below them was broken by a scattering of housing throughout the valley. Hard to imagine there was anyone else alive in the world. The place was so quiet.

"No cars or people. No sign of Frank North," sighed Gus.

"What do we do now?" asked Suzie.

"The logical place to look is inside that outbuilding."

"We need a warrant to get inside without an invitation."

"If they're up to no good and we walk down the hill and knock on the door…."

"They'd tell us to go away and disappear before we returned with a warrant."

"We'll leave it for today," said Gus, "Geoff Mercer can arrange surveillance tomorrow. If he's not back, I'll bend the ACC's ear until he does the necessary. I don't like the look of it, Suzie, but we can't jeopardise what might prove a major operation by jumping in too early. There could still be a simple explanation for Frank's disappearance."

They made the walk in silence. Gus stopped to stand on the bottom rung of gates at the entrance to the fields for any signs of Frank. A lone car passed them as it struggled up the incline.

"Two little old ladies out for a sunny Sunday afternoon drive," said Suzie.

"Seasoned criminals in Agatha Christie country," said Gus. "Sorry to interrupt your day with what turned out to be a waste of effort. Do you want to follow me back to my place? I can offer you a bowl of soup and a crusty roll."

"If you're sure I'm not keeping you from something important. Yes, please, the walk and the fresh air have made me hungry."

For the first time in a long time, two cars pulled into the driveway of Freeman's bungalow. They parked on the right-hand side, under the climbing roses.

"They're beautiful," said Suzie Ferris.

"My late wife Tess planted those. She hoped to trail them across the whole side of the bungalow in time."

"There's a long way to go, Gus, but they look sturdy enough."

"Bert Penman, one of my neighbours on the allotments near the church, reckons every plant has two choices. Live or die. Those roses are no different. I hope they continue to thrive because digging them up will mean one more memory of Tess gone."

"I haven't lost anyone close to me," said Suzie, "both my parents are going strong. We lost my maternal grandmother when I was eight. She lived in New Zealand with my grandfather. I was old enough to understand what had happened, but I'd never met her in person. So, it didn't have the same impact. Mum and Dad didn't take my brother and me out for the funeral, either. Too expensive. Gramps and my Dad's parents are in their eighties now and beginning to look frail."

They had moved inside the bungalow, and Gus showed Suzie into the lounge.

"Give me twenty minutes in the kitchen," he said, "see if there's anything among my record collection you fancy."

Gus got to work on the soup. Suzie called through from the next room: -

"Vinyl's making a comeback," she said, "you were right to hang on to these. You're in fashion again. My Dad's got a live Yardbirds album from the early Sixties he reckons is valuable. He treats it better than he treats my Mum."

"Not the one from the Marquee Club?" asked Gus, who stood in the doorway. "I've always wanted to find a copy of that. Clapton murdered the vocals on 'Good Morning Little Schoolgirl', but the album was sensational."

"It was a mono recording, so it sounds tinny compared to today's stuff. None of that was my scene, as you can imagine. Boyzone, Westlife and Britney Spears never got me hooked. I was only interested in horses."

"I guess it's not surprising if you live in this area. Where do you stable your horses?"

"I keep forgetting; you're new to this part of the county. We have a large farm near Worton, and the stables are a stone's throw from the main house. Horses have been part of my family for years. My Mum was a national champion, and my Dad rode point-to-point until recently. After that, music and several other things have taken a back seat to my horses and career."

"You're not related to Vera's family, are you?" Gus asked.

"Distant cousins," Suzie replied, "so you've delved into her background, have you?"

Gus grinned.

"I like to know who I'm working with," he said and returned to the kitchen to continue preparing lunch. Eva Cassidy's voice accompanied his labours. Eva was one of Tess's favourites.

"Is this too gloomy?" asked Suzie as she watched Gus pour the soup into two bowls. "I didn't think, sorry. My Mum loves listening to this album."

"We oldies can still pick them, then?" said Gus, inviting Suzie to sit. They ate in silence as the album moved track by track to the end of side one.

"That soup tasted great, Gus," said Suzie, "just what I needed. Do you want a hand with the washing-up?"

"Leave it. I'll put everything into the dishwasher. Are you rushing away?"

"What did you have in mind?

Gus missed the raised eyebrow. Instead, he was engrossed in getting the dishwasher stacked, as Tess insisted.

"It's still a pleasant afternoon," he said, "we could wander along to the allotments. You can thank my patch in person for its excellent vegetables."

"Exercise is always beneficial after lunch," said Suzie, "my Dad falls asleep in the chair by three o'clock. It's his age, I suppose."

"I never have that problem, young lady," said Gus, "now, are we ready?"

As they took a brisk walk through the village towards the allotments, Gus noticed neighbours in their gardens standing and staring. Other couples he didn't recognise strolling home from the pub nodded and said 'Hello'. Nobody took a blind bit of notice of him any other time.

Suzie Ferris slipped her arm through his.

"Now they'll have something to talk about," she laughed.

She let go of his arm when they reached the gateway to the allotments. Someone waved, eager to catch their attention.

"That's Bert Penman," said Gus, "the chap I mentioned. He's looking after my patch while I'm working on these cold cases. I wonder what he wants?"

"Afternoon, Mr Freeman," said Bert, removing his cap in the presence of a young lady. "afternoon, Miss."

"What's the matter?" asked Gus.

"There's something over yonder you need to see," said Bert, pointing to the far side of the allotments. Gus could see a young man who appeared to be comforting a woman, maybe his wife.

Gus started to run. Suzie chased after him. They saw a dark shape lying under the cemetery wall in the top corner of the field.

Gus recognised the overcoat and the worn-down soles of his shoes.

"Frank North."

"That degree of damage can only mean one thing," said Suzie Ferris.

"Two shots to the back of the head, execution-style," said Gus.

"I'll call it in. Do you know where Frank lives? Tell his wife. For God's sake, dissuade her from coming here. Whoever Monty Jennings has got involved with this time is bad news."

In **'Fatal Decision'**, Gus soon found his feet after three years in retirement. A murderer awaits sentencing, and another cold case file has landed on his desk..

The second book in the series **'Last Orders'** will follow.

Feel free to Tweet about any of my books, and please tell your friends about them. Every writer likes to receive a review; it's our lifeblood. If you can, then please do.

About The Author

Ted Tayler is the international best-selling indie author of the Freeman Files and Phoenix series. Ted lives in the English West country, where his stories are based. He was born in 1945 and has been married to Lynne since 1971. They have three children and four grandchildren.

His thought-provoking mysteries appeal to readers of Sally Rigby, Joy Ellis, Pauline Rowson, and Faith Martin. His action-packed thrillers are a must for fans of Mark Dawson and J C Ryan.

Gus Freeman's cold case investigations are carried out with reasoned deduction rather than bursts of frantic action. In each of the 24 books, unsolved murder is accompanied by romance, humour, and country life. The core message in the 12 Phoenix novels is that criminals should pay for their crimes. Unfortunately, the current system fails to deliver the correct punishment, so Phoenix helps redress the balance.

Acknowledgements

The love and support of my family; without them, this would have been impossible.

The Phoenix Club

Sign up to be on my mailing list for details of new adventures and the opportunities for receiving free books. You will receive a bonus copy of 'The Long Hard Road' for merely subscribing.

Sign up at - http://tedtayler.co.uk

Thanks again for reading. Until the next time.

Printed in Great Britain
by Amazon